Harrier Air War: 1985

Brad Smith

Copyright © 2018 Brad Smith

All rights reserved.

ISBN: 9781718194816

DEDICATION

To Maya and Hiro.

ACKNOWLEDGMENTS

Much of this book was written with the help of existing research and interviews about the Harrier GR.3. The most helpful of these sources was Bob Marston's "Harrier Boys" series. There was also a wealth of data about Harrier operations in wartime drawn from "The RAF Harrier Story", a collected series of lectures published by the Royal Air Force Historical Society.

1

Excerpt from The New York Times - Thursday May 2, 1985

US Destroyer Sunk in Gulf - World Tensions at All-Time High

An American destroyer sank near Bahrain yesterday, killing more than 60 American sailors, US Defense Department officials reported. The bodies of 67 crewmembers of the USS Arthur W. Radford have so far been recovered. Ongoing rescue efforts to locate the remaining 35 missing sailors are still underway as of press time.

Secretary of Defense Caspar Weinberger stated in a press conference that the ship was rocked by a series of explosions around 3:20 a.m. local time as the destroyer was on routine patrol approximately 35 miles off the eastern coast of Saudi Arabia. The secretary refused to speculate on the cause of the sinking.

The White House has opened an immediate investigation into the sinking. Naval investigators are scheduled to arrive in the area this morning. In his remarks to the nation on live television last night, President Reagan called the event "a national tragedy" and urged for "calm and prayer".

He also promised to take "swift and decisive action" against any nation or organization responsible for the sinking. Anonymous sources within the Defense Department say that the destroyer was likely torpedoed by a Soviet submarine believed to be operating in the area at the time of the sinking.

Moscow has denied having any part in the sinking of the Radford, stating in a short press release that "the tools of American imperialism have rightfully been paid back for the suffering they have caused around the globe."

Experts say the sinking, along with recent events in the region could significantly heighten the risks of a conflict involving the United States and the Soviet Union. The Arthur W. Radford was a Spruance-class destroyer that was visiting the Bahraini port as part of the US agreement to defend the country against potential Iranian military aggression.

Analysts say that tensions between the superpowers are at an all-time high due to a recent naval engagement between the two countries against the backdrop of a Soviet-supported invasion of Kuwait and Saudi Arabia that started on April 25.

The Iranians, who declared victory in their war with Iraq last year, annexed their neighboring nation last June and executed its head of state, Saddam Hussein. In January, Ayatollah Khomeini vowed in public statements that Iran would take revenge on the Gulf Council states for their support of Iraq during the war.

HARRIER AIR WAR: 1985

Iran began rebuilding and modernizing its military earlier this year with the help of Soviet aid and advisors.

Kuwait's surrender five days ago prompted the US State Department to issue an ultimatum for the Iranians to withdraw from the country immediately or face military action.

The Rapid Deployment Force was sent to Saudi Arabia to secure military airbases for American use. The US deadline for withdrawal expired without Iranian compliance and a US carrier task force was dispatched towards the Gulf from Diego Garcia.

Less than a day later, the Soviet ambassador warned it would take unspecified action against what it called "imperialistic meddling" in the region.

On April 28, US officials reported that a Soviet Kirov-class cruiser shadowing the American carrier group was sunk after firing its missiles at the carrier USS Kitty Hawk. The US carrier was undamaged and immediately retaliated with its full complement of attack aircraft.

The Soviets deny the Kirov attacked the carrier group and claim it was only acting in self-defense after an "unprovoked attack" by American warships.

Since then, US and Soviet diplomats have been expelled from each other's countries. An emergency closed-door United Nations meeting was held on April 29. A Canadian official who attempted to mediate the negotiations declared the meeting a "dismal failure".

Since the sinking of the Radford, NATO officials in Western Europe have increased their alert levels at airbases and ports throughout West Germany. US officials have begun activating reserve units in a move that Defense Department officials call "purely defensive" in purpose.

President Ronald Reagan has cancelled a planned upcoming trip to West Germany, stating that he would instead attend a state funeral to be held for the dead and missing sailors of the sunken destroyer. The services are scheduled for Monday and will be broadcast live on all major US television networks.

Despite appeals for calm by government officials, the American public has shown signs of increased anxiety over the growing possibility of war. Officials in several states have called for increased funding for civil defense. Pamphlets describing what to do in case of nuclear attack have been distributed among citizens in major cities including Atlanta, Miami, and San Diego.

Evacuation drills are expected to be held next week in Toledo, Cleveland, and Youngstown. Outlet stores in several locations throughout the US have experienced sporadic instances of "panic buying", completely running out of stock in a matter of days and, in some cases, mere hours after opening.

2

<u>May 2, 1985, 2000hrs</u>

RAF Gutersloh was busier than a five-ring circus tent on fire. Land Rovers full of ground crew and pilots rushed to and fro across the large grassy fields. Men in uniform and flight suits hurried among the base's low brown buildings. Tracked Rapier surface-to-air missile vehicles crawled towards their positions on the outskirts of the base.

Puma helicopters lumbered off noisily to their destinations. West German Tornado combat aircraft sped down the long runway, to patrol for any Warsaw Pact aircraft that might cross over the border to bomb NATO targets.

Located a little more than 100 kilometers southwest of Hannover, Gutersloh was a major NATO airbase that fell under the command of the Second Allied Tactical Air Force. 2ATAF, as it was commonly referred to, oversaw Gutersloh and all NATO airbases in its sector of operations. The major responsibility of 2ATAF was the air defense and support of NATO's Northern Army Group, NORTHAG for short.

NORTHAG consisted of a corps each from the armies of the British, Dutch, and West Germans for a total of three corps. This area consisted of a large chunk of western Europe that included Belgium, the Netherlands, and everything in West Germany north of the city of Kassel.

NORTHAG's main rivals across the East German border were both the Soviet 2nd Guards Tank Army and the 3rd Shock Army. The combined might of these two armies consisted of no less than seven corps.

Even with the technological and training advantage that NATO held over their adversaries to the east, the Soviet Union and Warsaw Pact's sheer weight in numbers would provide a real headache for the western defenders to contend with if the Soviet Union decided to move west.

Since Gutersloh was located a brisk five minutes' flight from the Inner German border, everyone there knew it would be one of the first installations to come under attack should a major war start in Central Europe.

To even the most hopeful of onlookers, this possibility seemed more real and imminent than it had in any other time since the end of World War Two only forty years ago.

NATO satellite and photo reconnaissance had picked up sure signs of mobilization across the board throughout Warsaw Pact countries. In response to these events, along with the growing crisis in the Middle East, NATO elevated its alert status to Orange level only three hours ago.

NATO commanders were somewhat certain that an

enemy attack was possible some time within the next 36 hours. Across western Europe, soldiers and vehicles were being deployed in defensive positions, warships were put out to sea, and senior officers were at their headquarters.

Although almost none of the men and women at Gutersloh had ever experienced a war first hand, the airbase itself was no stranger to conflict. Built in the 1930s for the Luftwaffe, it had withstood repeated bombings during the Second World War.

It was in April 1945 when the Americans captured the base that Gutersloh was finally removed from the quickly dwindling list of Nazi assets. Two months later, it was handed over to the RAF and ever since, it had played host to a long list of RAF squadrons that were rotated in and out as part of the UK's commitment to NATO.

Gutersloh was home to no less than four RAF squadrons, two of which - Number 3 and Number 4 Squadron - flew the Harrier GR.3. Each squadron had three flights of six Harriers each.

There were eight pilots per flight, two of whom would be able to take over the duties of anyone who was fatigued or shot down. The chance of something like the latter happening was quite high, as shown by the loss of two Sea Harrier and three Harrier GR.3 aircraft to enemy fire only a few years ago during the Falklands conflict.

Despite the losses, the Sea Harrier and Harrier GR.3 aircraft quickly became the stars of the conflict, grabbing the front-page headlines of nearly all the London tabloids. After the war ended and the Falklands had returned to British rule, the press briefly celebrated the planes and their pilots with the kind of admiration previously reserved for the Spitfire in the Battle of Britain.

Capable of vertical takeoff and landing (VTOL), the single-seat Harriers were regarded by the press and the public as futuristic marvels of military might. In truth, the aircraft were rapidly aging. Most of them had been built in the late 1960s and upgraded to the GR.3 version in the previous decade. Since then, nothing had changed.

Compared to the newer F-15 Eagles and F-16 Falcons recently introduced into the NATO air forces, the Hawker Harrier GR.3 was almost a dinosaur. The men who flew them, however, were well-trained and among the smartest and bravest of pilots in the RAF.

In the lonely silence of the Gutersloh mess hall tower, one Harrier pilot stood looking out the window feeling miserable. Squadron Leader James Hartley, call sign "Shadow", watched one of the Harriers in Number 3 squadron speed down the long runway and leap into the air on takeoff.

As the flight leader of the six Harriers in Shadow Flight, he couldn't wrap his head around why he was stuck here while the other two flights in the squadron had already left.

"Bloody unbelievable," he muttered to himself. "World War Three about to start and here we are entertaining the VIPs."

Hartley tugged hard in disgust at the bow tie around his neck and loosened the top button on his tunic. He unsnapped the clasps on the large window in front of him.

The whine of jet engines and helicopter rotors flooded into the room, no longer filtered by a window pane. It was good to feel the cool air against his face and smell the jet fuel burning in the planes outside.

He took a deep breath of dirty air and turned to find himself looking into the eyes of a young Hermann Goering. Hartley glared at the photo of the man in his World War I pilot days. He had to admit that Goering was quite dashing in his youth, before he became part of an inhuman regime that committed unspeakable acts.

Flying Officer Adam Nelson stepped in the room and appeared beside Hartley. The young man with his thin face and angular features turned and frowned at the sight of the photo. His call sign was "Horatio", a play on his last name. He had only been in the squadron for a few months and was the newest member of Shadow Flight.

"Wonder what old Goering would say about all this business outside." he said.

Hartley took a sip from his glass of ice water, wondering if it would have felt much different for a Luftwaffe pilot here on the eve of World War II. Despite the yawning gap between the political ideologies, those men had been humans too. The fear, frustration, and anticipation mingled together inside of him, making his leg tremble slightly.

"I'm sure he'd have a thing or two to say about why we were standing here in the biggest target in West Germany instead of dispersed to our Harrier hides anyway," he said.

"Are the other Harriers gone yet?" Nelson asked.

Hartley nodded. "The other two flights from Number 3 Squadron just left. There's only us now. All three flights from Number 4 Squadron departed ten minutes ago. I watched them all out."

Nelson sensed the frustration in Hartley's voice. He pointed to the photo. "Is it really true about Goering using this room to entertain the young Luftwaffe pilots back during the war?" he asked. He looked up at the wooden beams near the ceiling and squinted.

Hartley chuckled. "That's the rumor anyway," he said. "Fat bastard would come up here and tell a real corker about his old flying days. And then when he was finished impressing them, he'd say something like 'And if I'm lying, may God break the wooden beam above me'."

Hartley took Nelson by the shoulder and walked over to the corner of the room. A small wooden lever stuck out of the floorboards.

"What's this then?" asked Nelson, pointing to the lever.

"Goering would have an aide of his standing by to pull the lever right after he said those words," Hartley remarked. "The lever activated a rope holding a beam together on the ceiling. When it was pulled, the rope would loosen and the beam would appear to crack in two."

Hartley stared at Nelson, waiting for him to react to the joke. The young man didn't so much as flinch.

"I guess you had to be there," said Hartley. "Or maybe you have to be German," The sound of boots clomping up the stairs drummed loudly outside the room.

The door swung open and a red-haired giant ducked his head under the low archway of the door frame.

"Knackered. Thank god that's over with," said Warrant Officer Harold "Gandalf" Stewart. His Scottish brogue added a spice of fury to the words.

"How'd it go down there with the MP?" asked Hartley.

Stewart shrugged and rolled his eyes. "Ah'm pure scunnurt," he said. "We should be at our dispersal, sir. Not here. Bloody madness, if ye ask me." Stewart turned to the staircase where a series of off-notes were being sung. He rolled his eyes and closed the door.

Seconds passed and the door burst open again. A short and stocky young man bounded into the room, his smile full of playful energy. "Nobody expects the Spanish inquisition!" he shouted.

Stewart aimed a lazy kick at him that failed to land. "Spence, you're a right dobber. Ah saw you slippin' a dram inta tha man's bevvy."

The whole surreal evening finally clicked into place as Hartley realized the MP had begun acting progressively stranger throughout the dinner. His voice had become slurred and his Cockney accent more pronounced too. Stewart was probably right. The only explanation was the incorrigible "Jawsy" Spencer tampering with the man's drink.

Spencer laughed. "Come on, Stewart," he said. "I had to do something to liven up the evening. If we couldn't drink, then somebody had to drink our share for us."

"Spare us any more fun tonight, would you Spence?" asked Hartley. "It's been a long day even without the mandatory dinner tonight. Bloody hell, I mean.... ten training sorties."

Flight Lieutenant Harold "Hobbit" Bellamy walked in

next. He had the gentle looks and demeanor of a Man of Kent. His eyes were bright and kind and he had a round face that smiled too often.

Hartley told himself it was pure coincidence that he had two references to Tolkien among the pilots in his flight. But he wasn't quite sure that some Group Captain in charge of pilot assignments wasn't having a joke at Hartley's expense.

Bellamy playfully jabbed at Spencer and then walked over to Hartley. Holding a cigarette in one hand, he studied Hartley's face for a moment. "How are you getting on now?"

Hartley coughed and looked around the room. "Kate's gone back to live in London," he said. "The divorce was finalized last Friday. Bloody lawyers got their pay and finally buggered off. The house is like a ghost. I'm getting through it. Thanks."

Bellamy nodded and walked over to sit beside Stewart.

Squadron Leader Ryan Davis stepped through the door next, the expression on his face even more sour than usual. His uniform was pressed neatly and his boots spit-polished. The men joked that they were nearly blinded looking at the reflection of light coming off his shoes, thus giving him the call sign "Sunshine".

He was a tall man with a slender build. His neatly trimmed mustache and side-parted hair gave him an air of the "dashing" pilot from old black-and-white movies. He would have fit in perfectly beside Hermann Goering in the photo.

Hartley looked on with a mix of envy and pity at the

blue and green South Atlantic medal that Davis wore on his tunic. *You were on the way up after the war weren't you, Davis? Until that training accident anyway.*

Davis strode to the center of the room and brushed away invisible flecks of dust on his pristine dress uniform. "Why the hell haven't we been given the order to disperse yet? We're sitting ducks here, aren't we?" he demanded.

Hartley couldn't agree more with Davis but dared not say it aloud. The situation called for calm. He had bad news to deliver already and did not want to stoke the flames further. These were men under pressure.

He had already had a heated debate with Wing Commander Morrison on their arrival back from training earlier in the day. The squadron leader had pulled Hartley into his office and sat him down, explaining that a member of parliament was coming to Gutersloh and that orders were passed down to have a group of pilots for the VIP and his wife to talk with over a formal dinner in the mess.

Hartley had been incredulous at the suggestion and pointed out the need to disperse the six Harriers and eight pilots in the flight. They were on the verge of war and it was obvious that being here was dangerous and foolish. But the warped politics of Downing Street and decorum were at play here - reality be damned.

"Look, I know it's bloody inconvenient for you," Morrison had said apologetically. "He specifically wanted to talk to the Harrier pilots though. I can't very well say no, now can I? Besides, everyone else is too bloody busy."

And that, as they say, was that.

The MP had spent much of the dinner discussing the

UK commitment to NATO and its support for American policy in the Middle East. The eight Harrier pilots in Hartley's flight had sat there in polite discomfort for ninety long minutes listening to the man talk about issues about which he was surprisingly knowledgeable.

The long and short of it was that despite NATO's technological advantage, its main weakness was in its tenuous political alliances that were simultaneously kept together and pushed apart by a mixture of half-truths, bad history, and old rivalries. Had the MP come at any other time than tonight, Hartley reckoned he might have enjoyed the mini-lecture.

Instead it was kind of a torture knowing that the Harriers of Number 3 and 4 squadrons were being dispersed to their pre-designated hides away from the base. The hides were little more than clearings where the Harriers could operate from without the fear of being destroyed. NATO planners were fully aware that Warsaw Pact strike aircraft would be enthusiastically targeting NATO airbases during the early stages of any conflict.

To avoid detection by the enemy, the Harriers were camouflaged underneath the canopies of West Germany's lush forests or tucked away in its cities and towns.

"I have some bad news for us all," said Hartley. A chorus of groans came. "We will not be dispersing tonight. We'll be staying here at Gutersloh until the morning."

"Ya canna be serious!" shouted Stewart.

"Hell!" spat out Davis angrily.

Hartley appealed for calm. "I know you're as confused as I am about this decision," he said. "The word has come down from Morrison that our Harriers still need to undergo some important upgrades before they can be flown out in the morning. First light."

"Well, I suppose it's better than trying to find our hide in the dark," said Bellamy.

Hartley looked around the room. He suddenly realized he was missing two pilots. "Where are Dunhill and Martin?" he asked.

Davis pointed to the window. "Snuck out the dinner early and went to get sack time in the hangar," he said.

Hartley nodded. "Right then. We leave here at 0400 for the dispersal. The six of us take the Harriers. Dunhill and Martin will take a Puma to the site. Any questions?"

The room was quiet. A pall of quiet resentment and frustration hung heavy in the air.

"I suggest getting some sleep on the cots in the hangars," said Hartley finally. "With any luck, we'll wake up to find the alert level reduced. But I want you all to be ready for the real thing. Seconds will count."

Spencer's familiar laughter filled the room.

"Anything you care to share with us, Spence?" asked Hartley.

"Yes, sir," he said. "I was just wondering if I'll get back the rental fee for this uniform," said Spencer with a laugh. The rest of the room fell into a chorus of dull groans and chuckles.

"Be quiet! This is no joke! Spencer! Shut your gob,

man!" Davis shouted. An awkward silence filled the room.

Hartley glanced at Davis, unsure of whether to be grateful for his support this time.

"You've made me quite proud and we have earned the reputation as the squadron's best flight," said Hartley. "Let's keep it that way." He wanted so badly to inspire the men before him. He knew he was a good leader. Maybe not the most charming or the most cunning of men but certainly he was adequate. The men deserved better though.

Hartley searched for something else to say. Nothing came. It will have to do, I guess. "Right then! Dismissed!"

At that, Stewart sneezed loud enough to wake the dead. Hartley smiled and turned to Davis. "Thank you...," he stammered. Davis strode off towards the door without acknowledging him.

"You wee bastard!" Stewart shouted.

Hartley suppressed a smile. Stewart stood there covered in talcum powder, wiping away at the white splotches that covered his lower face and tunic.

Spencer, the one who had proffered Stewart the napkin with talcum powder tucked inside the folds, was nearly doubled over in laughter. Stewart shouted at the younger man, his brogue too thick and fast to understand. He took an angry step towards Spencer, who backed up out of the room and ran down the spiral staircase.

Hartley turned his eyes back to the window, watching the lights of the long runway blink on and off as planes took off and landed.

Nelson and Bellamy stayed in the room chatting in low tones about the day's sorties.

"Nice hits with the ADENs," Bellamy said to Nelson. "Just make sure you slow down and make short bursts. Watch the tracers. Not the HUD. Those cannons are notoriously inaccurate. You're getting much better, you know."

Nelson thanked him for the compliment and the two men walked out of the room together, talking about low level cluster bomb approaches.

Hartley was alone in the room. He glared again at the photo of Herman Goering. A cold excited shiver ran down his spine. For all his bluster, experienced aviators knew that Goering's tales were bullocks. Heroism only happened when men worked together.

The brotherhood of pilots who trained and worked together was the only thing that mattered up in the air. If war came, it would be the bonds among the men that kept them alive. Were his men ready? Had he forged them into a team that could not only survive but accomplish their goals? Only the real thing would tell him that.

Hartley left the room completely unaware of how soon his questions would be answered.

3

Hartley bolted upright in his cot. His body was up and moving before his brain was even aware of it. The sirens on the base screamed out for him. The other pilots arose with a stream of loud curses of shock and anger. The lights in the hangar shone blood red.

Hartley knew instantly the NATO alert level had just increased from Orange to Scarlet level. Enemy activity was expected within minutes. War was here. It was time to get out of Dodge, as the Americans say.

With his brain on fire and his legs and heart slamming blood back and forth, he picked up his flight helmet and slapped it on his head. The ground crew was ready and a runner stepped forward with a sealed envelope. Hartley took it and adjusted his helmet strap. The slapping of boots on pavement echoed throughout the hangar. The other men in the flight were rushing to their Harriers.

The aircraft technician looked up at him and nodded with his thumb up. Hartley nodded back and clambered up the short ladder that took him to his Harrier cockpit. He sat down in the cramped cockpit and ripped open the envelope marked WARLOC, short for "War Locations".

Inside were a series of maps and notes that showed the location of the Harrier dispersal sites, complete with approach vectors and radio frequencies. Hartley slid one of the maps onto his kneeboard.

There was no time to program the location into his navigation computer. He would have to fly by instrument and reckoning, which was fine. He and his men had trained for such things many times.

The first and only priority was to get off the ground immediately. If the Russians were indeed on the way, they would be loaded for bear and ready to drop bombs on his position. Hartley stepped into the cockpit and sat down, switching on the electrical power. The Harrier's Pegasus engine started up with its high-pitched whine.

As the engine spooled up, Hartley glanced over to see Nelson and Bellamy begin their taxi towards the runway. When he got outside of the hangar, Hartley was relieved to see Stewart, Spencer, and Davis in their Harriers doing the same. He rolled along the taxiway for a short time and then cut over the grassy field for the middle of the runway.

It would have been impossible for a modern fighter jet to take off with such a short strip of pavement - but not for Harriers. What gave these planes their vertical takeoff and landing ability were four side-mounted nozzles, through which fast-moving air could push against the body of the aircraft.

A lever in the cockpit gave Harrier pilots the ability to rotate the nozzles. For the Harrier's customary short take off, Hartley pointed the nozzles down to add lift to the plane. Hartley's aircraft rolled down the runway and lifted up after only a dozen or so meters.

"Shadow One to Shadow Flight, confirm your status," Hartley said as the ground fell away below him. The other three pilots radioed back that they were in the air and joining formation. Hartley allowed himself to relax a little. There was a sliver of deep purple light on the horizon. A look on his watch showed the time. It was 0407.

Without warning, Gutersloh exploded behind him. In the early morning darkness, the base erupted in flame and destruction. Ground technicians and crew directing aircraft on the flight line were incinerated by the initial blasts and concussion. The Tornadoes and Phantoms on the taxiway were gone in an instant.

One of the Phantoms caught on the runway was flipped over violently in the air from the nearby explosions. The fuel in the aircraft was quickly consumed by the bright orange flames.

The ordnance was next. A rack of five-hundred-pound iron bombs exploded, leaving a deep crater in the ground. The hardened hangars were spared the worst of it. Their thick steel doors were closed just before the missiles reached the airbase.

"Jesus…," Hartley said. He watched in his mirror as the place he had worked, trained, and played was engulfed in flame.

Hartley dialed the frequency for the AWACS airborne early warning aircraft circling far to the west. "Shadow to Eyes, give me an intercept," he said into the radio. No response. Unlike the Sea Harrier, the Harrier GR.3 had no radar though it did have a radar warning receiver.

The pilot was aware of a threat's existence and usually what type of threat he faced but not exactly where it was in relation to him.

Hartley cursed and called out to his flight on the radio. "Shadow Flight let's not waste any time. Head for the dispersal area immediately. Stay low." A chorus of shocked affirmatives met him. *Well, at least I can bloody well communicate with my own flight.*

Seconds later, Hartley's radar warning receiver chirped. Somewhere out there nearby was a search radar. Looking up out of the bubble canopy, he spotted the unmistakable triangular shape of a MiG-21 silhouetted against the faint light of the pre-dawn sky. The enemy plane's afterburner glowed like a cigarette in a dark room. Another MiG followed close behind.

"Bandits!" he called out to his flight. "I have a pair of MiGs up there heading west. Angels 3 at two o'clock."

It was time to decide. Should he press on towards the hide or engage the bandits? The Harriers were all armed with a pair of AIM-9 Sidewinders. The MiGs were moving fast towards the west and clearly on a mission to destroy NATO forces. The Harriers couldn't keep up a pursuit against the much faster enemy aircraft. The chance likely wouldn't come again. The choice seemed already made for him.

"Let's engage those MiGs," he said to the flight.

Hartley pushed the throttle forward. The Harrier responded immediately to his control input and leapt into the sky. The MiGs overflew Gutersloh from the east. Anti-aircraft fire from near the base's security perimeter sparked up around the enemy aircraft. Hartley's plane was close behind. The tracers from the anti-aircraft guns leapt up all around his cockpit.

"Watch out for that AAA!" yelled Hartley. It suddenly occurred to him that he might just as well be shot down or killed by his own side on the first day of the war. *Shot down by friendly fire. Not something I want on my tombstone.*

The MiGs dipped low towards the airbase. Hartley noticed the undercarriages were loaded with iron bombs, no doubt aiming for the runway. As he turned in behind them, he tried to lock the Sidewinder's radar onto the lead plane.

He watched the circle on his heads-up display drift towards the MiG bomber. The enemy pilot didn't even flinch as the AIM-9 locked onto him. The low growl of the missile radar turned into a high-pitched tone indicating a good lock. Hartley fired.

The missile shot forward from his Harrier, a thin trail of smoke pouring from its exhaust. The MiG pilot angled slightly to the left in a feeble attempt to evade but the missile caught up quickly and exploded right behind him. The bomber's rear fuselage disintegrated in mid-air and the front of the plane became a twirling fireball that tumbled towards the ground.

The other MiG continued its dive towards the tarmac. Hartley breathed hard and switched to guns. *This one's stubborn.* The aiming reticle on his HUD came to life and he steered the Harrier's nose towards the rear of the enemy plane. Just before he squeezed the trigger, he watched in horror as the MiG's bombs fell from its wings.

Too late. Bastard! Hartley felt the sweat bead on his

forehead as the gun ripped into the enemy aircraft's vertical stabilizer. The MiG pulled up and to the left with its afterburners on full.

Hartley kept his finger down and the 30mm cannon rounds slammed hard into the MiG's fuselage. He watched it roll over slowly as if it were an animal gracelessly dying in mid-flight. A second later, he was past the crippled MiG and it crumpled straight into the ground below.

"Good kill! Good kill!" shouted Nelson.

There was a long silence. Finally, an AWACS controller spoke to him. "Eyes to Shadow Three One. Friendlies are at five miles, angels four, heading 270," he heard. The voice sounded very far away and there was much more static than usual. Hartley wondered if it was due to electronic jamming. Nothing seemed to be working right with communications this morning.

"Shadow Three One to Flight," said Hartley. "Be advised we have friendlies inbound."

Hartley kept the Harrier low and on a vector for the hide.

The radar warning receiver lit up again. A low buzz sounded in his ear.

The buzzing became louder and more shrill with each passing second. "I'm locked up. Engaging defensive!" Hartley banked and rolled the Harrier. Alarms rang in his ears. An enemy missile had been launched and was out there trying to find him.

Hartley jerked the flight stick hard left and let out a stream of chaff and flare from the aircraft, hoping it would be enough to act as a decoy for the approaching enemy missile.

"Are these the friendlies you were telling us about?!" said Davis.

"Someone's locked me up!" shouted Bellamy. "Engaging defensive!"

"My transponder says they're friendly!" shouted Stewart.

"Request permission to engage." It was Nelson. His voice was eerily calm and cool.

Hartley brought the plane low to the ground. His view out the canopy on his left was filled with the rolling hills of West Germany. He keyed his radio. "Do not engage! I repeat, do not engage."

Hartley grunted and felt the blood drain from his head as he pulled a six G turn and pointed the nose down below the horizon. He clenched his muscles during the turn and hoped he wouldn't pass out. The radar warning beeped steadily.

"I'm hit!" shouted Bellamy. "Ejecting!"

Hartley made another tight turn. A second later, the enemy missile passed no more than a dozen meters above him. He breathed a sigh of relief as he brought the Harrier level. The nearby hilltops were above his aircraft. The Harrier skimmed the treetops mere feet below. Hartley glanced at his altimeter. It indicated double digits.

"Fer Christ's sake, they shot down Hobbit!" said Stewart.

"I just spoke with Eyes," said Davis. "Those were F-15s. The AWACS called them off us."

"You bastards!" shouted Stewart. "We're on your side!"

Hartley tried to shelve his anger and grief by focusing on flying his plane. He brought the Harrier back up to a more reasonable altitude of 150 feet, skimming over the dark forest canopies of the North German plain below.

"Shadow Flight, we are RTB," Hartley radioed to his men.

They turned north and flew at treetop level for the hide.

4

The Harrier hide was nothing more than a group of Land Rovers, trucks, and Marshall cabin box-bodied vehicles in a small plot of unused farmland next to a grove of trees. The steel planks on the ground served as a makeshift taxiway.

Once the Harriers landed in the clearing, they drove a short way along the planking and arrived under a canopy of trees. From here, the Harriers could taxi out the other side of the clearing and take off by using a nearby paved local access road. It was just like camping - only with bombs and rockets and million-pound jet aircraft.

Hartley sat in his cockpit and watched the technicians help unload the supply trucks onto carts and wheel them towards the Harriers. Hartley couldn't quite believe it. He had just parked the plane thirty seconds ago and his Harrier was already being prepped for a mission.

One of the ground crew climbed up and handed Hartley his customary soda and chocolate bar. It was 0425, the sun was still not up yet, and the sugary breakfast tasted exquisite.

The remaining four Harriers landed nearby. The missing Harrier was a painful reminder of Bellamy's loss. The question lingered in Hartley's mind as to how the men in his flight would deal with it.

He had trained hard with the men and knew they were very capable. But the reality of combat was here and the losses were real. Would they crack? It was time to talk face-to-face and see how they were doing.

Hartley finished his chocolate bar then wiped his kneeboards with his sleeves. He folded the maps away then climbed out of the cockpit. The cool early morning air felt wonderful and the adrenaline still pulsed through his body. He hopped down off the ladder and heard his name called. Turning towards the source, he spotted Briscoe, the operations officer for the squadron.

Hartley smiled faintly at seeing the man, suddenly remembering his reference to Briscoe during last night's dinner with the MP. Hartley had tried several times to explain the various roles in the squadron using military parlance only to receive a blank look in return. Finally, he had resorted to using sports analogies.

"I suppose you could liken it to rugby league," he had tried to explain. "In regard to my flight, I would be the team captain. The operations officer - that's Briscoe - would be the coach, and the squadron leader, Wing Commander Morrison, would be the team owner." The analogy wasn't anywhere near perfect, but it was close enough to help the MP absorb the concept.

Hartley walked over to Briscoe with his head down, bracing himself for bad news like a slap in the face. Briscoe held up a cup of tea. "Brew?" he asked. Hartley shook his head.

"What's the latest?" said Hartley.

"Gutersloh is gone," Briscoe said. "SCUD missiles. There was nothing anyone could do about it. Last reports say they were hit with chemicals and high explosives. We've lost contact with them now."

"And the others?" Hartley asked.

Briscoe shook his head. "All of the big bases were hit," he said. "Initial estimates say Rammstein, Bitburg, and Rhein-Main are all offline. The rest? We don't know yet. So much jamming and confused reports flying around. It's hard to know what to believe. It's a ball of chalk, all around. Everyone's going on what we were told would happen rather than what's really going on out there."

"What if they're two completely different things?"

Briscoe had no answer for him.

"How about the other two flights? Safe and sound?"

Briscoe nodded and folded his arms. "They're staying put but not for long," he said. "We've got reports of armor pushing hard towards Bremen and Hannover. The West Germans are falling back towards the Weser.

"British I Corps has moved up into position but can't seem to find the main axis of attack. They will soon, I'm sure. I imagine it'll be a busy day. Plenty of work for everyone. When the sun comes up, anyways."

Hartley stepped aside as two ground crewmembers

wheeled a cluster bomb towards his Harrier. "We lost Bellamy," he said.

"Sorry. I know. I heard," said Briscoe. "Friendly fire. There's been a lot of that this morning. Won't be the last of it, either."

It was small comfort for Hartley. The other four pilots in the flight strode towards one of the Marshall cabins. Briscoe nodded to the men as they passed. "Morning," he said. But for a few replies of "Sir", they were silent. Stewart closed the door behind them.

Briscoe lit a cigarette and took a sip from his tea. "How are they handling it?" he asked.

Hartley shook his head. "Don't know yet, really," he said. "Bellamy was a big loss. Getting killed by friendly fire somehow makes it even worse. I know it shouldn't matter but it does."

He lit a cigarette and stood quietly with Briscoe. Above them in the faint pre-dawn light, the skies were filled with the sounds of jet aircraft on their way to assigned targets. It was impossible to guess which were friendly or enemy. Hartley guessed that the pilots up there had the same problem.

There was a huge air traffic jam above Central Europe and Shadow Flight had already had a bitter taste of the results. Hartley thought about what he might do if he ever found the pilot that shot down Bellamy.

A violent urge welled up from somewhere deep within him and then settled immediately. *No. It was a mistake. It may have been careless or even negligent. But in the end, it was a mistake. Murder won't bring back Bellamy.* Hartley threw the cigarette butt down and crushed it with his boot.

"Dunhill and Martin make it here yet?" asked Hartley.

Briscoe smiled faintly. "Their helo went down on the way here," he said. "Don't worry. They're fine. They managed to get hold of civilian transport and are making their way here now."

A wave of relief wash over Hartley.

"Well, we'd better get in there," said Briscoe. "I have a telebriefing to give the other flights at 0450."

The two men walked into the cabin. Maps of the NORTHAG sector were lined along its walls. An old worn folding table sat in the middle of the cabin where the five pilots of Shadow Flight sat. They said nothing to each other. Stewart lit a cigarette and stared down at the table in quiet rage.

"Gentlemen, let me start off first by offering my deepest sympathies about Bellamy," said Briscoe. "He was an important member of our family and the way it happened makes it even more difficult to accept. We still have a job to do, however, and it's important to focus on what needs to be done.

The enemy has pushed through in force all along the border as of 0400," he said. "The Americans in the south are withdrawing slowly but in good order. Here in the north, we're not having the same kind of luck. British I Corps and West German I Corps are holding near the border, but the Belgians are in some disarray. I expect we'll be busy south of Hannover this morning."

"To the south, the American defenders have a natural

advantage due to the hilly and mountainous terrain of southern Germany," said Briscoe. "Up here, we don't have any of that.

The only natural barriers are the major rivers, of which there are three. Going from east to west, we have the Weser, the Emse, and the Rhine. Our general plan is to lead the enemy west with a fighting withdrawal while eliminating most of the crossing points and bridges."

Briscoe pointed to the map, showing the location of each major river. "We'll keep a few bridges of our choosing intact to funnel their forces towards defensive strong points. This will cause the enemy to concentrate their forces together at key crossing points. When that happens, the air forces will focus their maximum destructive power at those points. Questions?"

Davis raised his hand. "Sir, what if the ground forces are unable to hold on against the advance long enough for us to work effectively?"

"That's where you'll be coming in," said Briscoe. "You are to help ensure that the enemy stays where he should be until we decide it's time for him to advance. We want to control what the enemy does, where he does it, and when. The key to all that is effective use of airpower. To that end, I expect you'll be performing interdiction and close air support for most of the day."

Briscoe pointed to the blackboard where the day's weather forecast showed sunny skies with light winds a ground temperature of 14 degrees. "Should be a nice one if you're going on a family picnic or starting World War Three," he said. No one laughed. "I'll be back to brief you later if there aren't any questions."

The room was deathly silent. "Right," he continued. "I expect we'll have some work for you to do very soon. Please take some time to get a cup of tea and go for a stretch but don't wander out too far. The pongos guarding us are tense and liable to shoot first and ask questions later."

Briscoe walked out of the cabin.

The five men sat sullenly at the table. Nelson's face was streaked with tears. Hartley tried to relax with a few slow deep breaths. He hoped the right words would come. They didn't.

Stewart cursed and muttered to himself. Hartley knew enough to let the young Scot brood for a while before saying anything. Nelson folded his arms and kept staring down at the surface of the table. Spencer got up quietly and stood staring at the maps on the wall. The shock seemed not to have worn off. Hartley waited for it to pass.

Stewart struggled to light a cigarette. On his third attempt, the metal-cased lighter gave up and simply refused the flame. The big red-haired man tossed it onto the table in disgust. "Fucking shite," he said. Hartley extended his own light and the big man nodded in thanks as he greedily puffed on his cigarette.

"This is really happening," said Spencer finally. "I can't quite believe it. What if it goes nuclear? I suppose we're all finished then."

The question lingered there among the smoky cabin.

Davis took a sip of hot tea. "We'll take more before the day's out," he said. "We'd better be prepared for that. Just do it as we've been trained and come home safely. That's

HARRIER AIR WAR: 1985

the way."

Hartley started to worry about the strain showing among the men already. Then he pushed it out of his mind. *They're professionals. They'll keep it together.*

Ten minutes later, they were back in the cockpits of their Harriers. Briscoe's runner came out with a map that showed the rough position of the frontline and the target. Hartley started marking it off in grease pencil. Thankfully, the waypoints to and from the target were already entered into the aircraft's notoriously finicky navigation system.

"Battlefield air interdiction west of Wolfsburg," Hartley radioed the other members of the flight. He finished his pre-flight and heard the groundcrew attaching cluster bombs to the wing pylons. One of them was covered in chalk and read "Bob's Your Uncle." The markings on another bomb got straight to the point. "Piss off Ivan!" it read.

Hartley was pleased with the mission assignment. The Harrier was at its best when assigned to hit targets just behind enemy lines. It was a very dangerous job to attack well-protected units in the rear, but it was much preferable to the confusion of close air support missions. Such missions were flown in very close proximity to friendly forces so there was the added stress of trying to avoid inflicting casualties on friendlies.

Even at low altitude, the Harrier would be flying too fast to visually identify one tank as friendly and another as enemy. Such missions were much better flown by dedicated air support aircraft like A-10s or attack helicopters such as the new Apache.

The details came in over the radio. Hartley mentally

jotted them down. The fighting to the east of Hannover was at a stalemate. The British Army on the Rhine along with the Belgians were just barely clinging on.

During its most recent reconnaissance flight, a group of Harriers from No. 4 squadron had found a battalion-sized group of Soviet tanks and vehicles trundling over the West German border behind the 3rd Shock Army.

A recce team had moved into the area less than ten minutes ago and pinpointed the enemy battalion's position. Apparently, they were using a two-lane highway to move west after crossing the Inner German border.

Intelligence estimated that these were latecomers from the 12th Guards Tank Division.

Hartley nodded to himself, agreeing with the estimate. *Too small to be a follow-on force. Must be someone late to the party.*

The Harriers of Shadow Flight were to destroy the tanks and stop them from reinforcing the Soviet force already engaged in battle at the front. If they moved quickly enough, they could stop the enemy vehicles before they reached Wolfsburg.

Hartley thought about the low-altitude bombing runs that the cluster munitions would demand. There would be AAA and ground fire to worry about, not to mention the need for top cover.

Artillery had been assigned to hit the long column of tanks and men. It was long range and not very accurate, but it would hopefully keep the heads of the AAA gunners and hand-held SAM operators down just long enough to make a good bombing run.

Dutch F-16s were provided for air escort. Hartley tried to suppress a bitter laugh. *I hope these gentlemen know what a Harrier looks like when they see one.*

After finishing his checks, the ground crew cleared him and the rest of Shadow Flight for takeoff. Once in the air, they flew north and circled. The men were mostly quiet over the radio as they waited for their escorts to arrive. Spencer chattered on for a few minutes until Hartley declared radio silence. The Dutch pilots were due to arrive in less than three minutes.

Seven minutes later, the planes had arrived.

5

Hartley got on the comms channel and spoke directly to the Dutch pilots.

"Prowler Flight, this is Shadow Flight, glad to have you with us, over." Hartley noted that only three of the four F-16s had arrived.

He thought of asking about it and then pushed the thought out of his mind. *Maybe one of them had mechanical failure.* But he knew better.

The escorting F-16s flew above him at medium altitude. It was a compromise between being targeted by SAMs and AAA.

He threw his throttle forward as the nozzles swept back. Soon the Harriers would be keeping pace with the fighters.

"Shadow Flight, we're sorry for the delay in arriving," said the Dutch lead pilot. "We ran into some surprise guests on the way to the party."

Stewart chimed in. "No worries, mate. We've got nothin' better ta do than hang around here, really."

Hartley smiled as he listened to the confused response from the Dutch pilot. "Sorry, Shadow Flight. Not reading you there. Say again?"

"Well, we're just glad to have you with us," Hartley said, trying his best to sound sincere.

"Actually, we're nearly Winchester at this point," came the reply. "We're hoping we don't run into too many problems over the target area."

Hartley's heart sank. Bloody hell. *What good are you with a couple of missiles? There are a thousand aircraft out there.*

He bit his lip and keyed his transmitter. "Roger that, we'll try to keep our time over target short enough. If there's any trouble, let us know and we'll RTB."

He didn't want to have to return to base but if the Dutch pilots ran into problems he would do it. An unarmed Harrier was no match for any air threats that might appear.

There was nothing more to say. The radio fell silent. The five remaining Harriers in Shadow Flight skimmed the trees at low altitude, heading northeast towards Hannover. The North German Plain unfolded below them with its green fields and twisting rivers and tributaries.

Hartley's radar warning receiver lit up as they neared Hannover. It was no surprise. The amount of military hardware around the area was bound to be impressive.

As he flew over a small hill, a short burst of AAA

tracers popped up past his right wing. He shrugged. *More friendly fire.*

Hartley looked to his left and saw the enormous cloud of smoke and dust just to the east and south of Hannover. The front lines were easy to spot by the black columns of burning tank fuel and oil. Flashes of artillery lit up the ground here and there.

Hartley felt grateful he wasn't flying into that hell with no visibility and all that ground fire trying to shoot him down. He watched a pair of A-10 tank-killer aircraft swoop low over the fields and disappear into the plume of smoke and fire.

He suddenly snapped out of it when he heard the voice of an F-16 pilot on his radio. "Shadow Flight, be advised. We're picking up some enemy air traffic ahead. Might want to slow down on your approach while we thin the herd a little for you."

Hartley brought the throttle back and looked behind him as the rest of the Harriers in formation reduced their speed. Somewhere near them were enemy aircraft just waiting to pounce on his Harriers.

Ten seconds later, one of the Dutch pilots called out the distance and range to a pair of MiG-21s. "Engaging!" he heard one pilot shout.

"Fox Two!" shouted another.

He looked up to see an AIM-7 Sparrow leave the weapons pylon on one of the Falcons. It dropped for a moment and then the engine sparked up and pushed the missile east. A few seconds later, the destruction of the enemy plane was announced by the sudden appearance of a small fireball off in the distance.

"Splash one. That's a kill!" he heard.

The lead F-16 pilot radioed in. "Let's tighten up. Be careful with your remaining missiles. Use guns if you can."

Hartley slowed the Harrier down and started a long lazy circle. The fields and forests lay just below him. He glanced to his right and caught a flash of movement. He squinted hard and saw a pair of Hind helicopters lumbering to the east less than a kilometer away. Hartley couldn't believe his luck.

"Shadow this is Gandalf," he heard over his radio. It was Stewart and his thick deep Scottish brogue snapped Hartley to attention. "I've got a pair of Hinds at your three. Request permission to engage."

Hartley knew how deadly the Hinds were to NATO ground troops and vehicles. They were killing machines armed with anti-tank missiles, rockets, and heavy machine guns. These were platforms that were designed for efficient close-range low altitude killing. If he did nothing and let the Hinds reach the front, they could deal a very deadly blow to the NATO defenses.

"Shadow Leader to Flight, engage," Hartley responded. "Let's spring the trap just like we did in training."

Hartley made a rough estimation of how long it would take for the Hinds to arrive near him. He found a clearing and dropped to a height only a few meters from the ground. The Harrier's nozzles pointed down and the nose was aimed into the wind. Nelson sat beside him in his own Harrier, hovering and waiting.

To the east, Stewart and Davis flew behind the helicopters, circling around them and threatening them with the occasional burst of cannon fire. Spencer sat with his Harrier hovering just to the west of where Harley and Nelson lay in wait.

The Hinds were unknowingly being herded towards Hartley and Nelson with the bonus of Spencer as bait. The big helicopters pushed ever closer to Hartley's position, all the while gaining speed and altitude as they panicked.

Hartley waited in the clearing with Nelson, listening to Spencer talk excitedly on the radio.

"Shadow this is Jawsy, they're heading right for you! Any second now!"

Hartley heard the rotors of the big helicopters as they approached the clearing. The first one passed right above where Nelson sat and the second one followed close behind. Hartley couldn't help but smile as he brought the Harrier up with its nose pointed towards the rear of the Hinds. At point blank range, the Harrier's ADEN cannons tore into the rear of both enemy helicopters.

The lead Hind tilted left at the impact of the cannon rounds. The pilot overcorrected, swinging the helicopter dramatically to the right and into the path of the trailing Hind. The second pilot had no time to react as his helicopter slammed into the first. The rotors broke and spun off in all directions.

The tail of the lead Hind folded in half and plummeted, dragging the rest of the helicopter with it. Both Hinds hit the treetops and disappeared under the forest canopy. Seconds later, thick black smoke curled up from where they had crashed.

Hartley and Nelson brought their Harriers back into formation. "Shadow Flight, good show." Even Spencer was struck speechless by what had just happened. Hartley felt justifiably proud. *Just like we had trained to do all these years.*

A sobering glance at the indicators showed the Harrier's low fuel status. They were getting close to bingo fuel and would need to conduct their mission soon and head for home. Hartley snapped his radio net back to the F-16s.

"Shadow Flight, you're clear for approach over target," he heard. The tense voice of the F-16 pilot said. "Be advised we are Winchester." The F-16 escorts had no more air-to-air ordnance.

"Should probably turn back," said Davis.

Hartley looked at his map and computed the distance to the target. They were so close right now. He breathed in hard and aimed the aircraft east. "Shadow Flight, proceed towards target." Soon they were behind the frontlines.

Hartley patched into the ground commander's radio network. A small recce team had been shadowing the battalion from a distance. They gave him the battalion's precise location. Hartley made the mark on his map with a grease pencil and adjusted his waypoint.

"Shadow Flight, Let's do things just as we trained. Let's hit them all at once from everywhere at once," he said. "Gandalf and Jawsy hit the rear. I'll go up the middle and hit the front. Sunshine and Horatio come in from the sides and hit the middle."

He swung the Harrier over and brought the plane along the Bundesstrasse, the big highway heading east-to-west where he was assured he would find the column of enemy tanks and vehicles.

Hartley considered the work that would come. The cluster bombs would need to be dropped at low altitude for the munitions to have any effect. If the mission was to have any meaning, they would need to keep low and fly level.

As the flight the highway, Hartley listened to the radio, waiting to hear back from the forward controller. There was only silence. Where the hell is the artillery?

If they were going to hit the column, it had to be now. With no real air cover and with the fuel low, they were desperately short of time.

Davis came over the radio. "We can't hit that thing without any anti-air suppression!" he shouted.

Hartley kept flying on towards the target, desperately hoping to hear the artillery was on the way already. Nothing. There was no time left.

"Shadow Flight, engage enemy ground targets," he said.

Davis came back on. "You can't be serious!"

The Harriers behind him split off into their assigned attack patterns.

Hartley flew straight down the highway towards the tanks at 540 knots. The radar warning blare and a puff of smoke drifted upwards. He snapped the Harrier to the right and a SAM passed mere feet above his cockpit.

The AAA came next, heavy and thick. Hartley rolled back to the horizon and pitched up and down, hoping to confuse the fire control radar just enough to evade the enemy fire.

Far ahead of him, Stewart and Spencer crossed over the rear of the target at the same time and released their cluster bombs. As they fell, the bombs broke up into tiny submunitions. Each of the hundreds of bomblets exploded as they landed. They flashed like a string of giant firecrackers. The bombs detonated on the thin top armor plating of the tanks and infantry fighting vehicles.

The rain of destruction they unleashed was beautiful to watch from up in the plane. Trucks and jeeps blew up instantly, their burning fragments splashing outwards. Infantry carriers shattered under the fiery blossom of direct hits.

Less than a second later, Davis and Nelson crisscrossed the highway near the middle of the enemy column. The submunitions fell and the hapless vehicles underneath were caught in a lake of flaming destruction as the bomblets scattered over them and exploded.

A SAM missile leapt up from somewhere near the side of the column. It lashed out towards Stewart's plane as he banked left to avoid a thick stream of flak.

Stewart rolled his Harrier and brought it into a tight turn, hoping to turn inside the missile's radar envelope. With any luck, the missile would lose its lock on him and fly past. No good. There was a flash and the rear fuselage of his Harrier was simply gone.

"Gandalf here. I'm hit!" he heard over the radio.

Hartley watched in horror as his plane pancaked into the nearby field and then skid into the woods to the north.

Hartley suddenly noticed he was too high to drop his cluster bombs. He brought his nose back down towards the pavement and prayed that Stewart would be alright. Hang in there, mate.

The radar warning receiver chirped and then came a series of beeps. Hartley couldn't see the SAM launch, but he knew the missile was out there. He yanked the throttle back and jinked the aircraft hard left, letting out chaff and flare behind him. A second later, there was a sharp sudden bang behind him.

At first, Hartley was convinced he had been hit. The Harrier shuddered and whined. The display on the central warning system lit up in orange. He struggled with the controls as the plane started to spin and gently descend. A heartbeat later, he had the plane back under his control though he felt the aircraft shuddered as it gained speed.

The HUD showed the bombsight on the lead vehicles of the column. Hartley resisted the urge to pull up, keeping the Harrier as steady as possible as the cluster bombs dropped from his wings. The Harrier lightened as he pickled the bombs over top the lead vehicles.

A vehicle-mounted anti-aircraft gun *clackclackclacked* at him as he rolled hard right to get away from the formation of enemy ground troops and tanks. As he pulled straight up, the aircraft was buffeted by a series of bumps. Behind him, the cluster bombs exploded. He punched the throttle and the engine whined a high-pitched protest as the Harrier picked up speed.

A minute later, he was heading south at low altitude

with two Harriers in tow. Hartley bit his lip and hoped the remaining Harrier would be joining them soon enough.

"Shadow Flight, check in," he said.

Nelson chimed in over the comms. "Shadow this is Horatio, No sign of Jawsy."

Hartley couldn't believe it. *How could I have possibly missed a man getting shot down in my own flight?*

So much had happened in a flash. His head was still spinning and the adrenaline was flooding his body. His first instinct was to turn the flight around and head back to help rescue the men. But a look at his fuel gauge and the holes in his fuselage were enough to convince him that it was out of the question.

Hartley saw the warning lights on in the cockpit and looked in the mirror. The airframe had several holes poking through it. But there was no sign of any smoke or flames. The stick felt heavy and though he was flying in a potential deathtrap, he kept going anyways.

The only comfort was the fact that the Mark 9 ejection seat in which he sat would instantaneously blow out of the cockpit when the handles were pulled. Hartley kept flying with an occasional glance backwards to check for signs of trouble developing.

"Did anyone get a marker on Gandalf?" he asked. Nelson gave him an estimate of Stewart's position. Hartley checked his map then relayed the coordinates to the air commander.

A few minutes later, word came back that the recce team had spotted a parachute from a doomed Harrier that had been nailed by a SAM. The team was on its way to the crash site.

Hartley's heart sank, knowing that the chance of safely ejecting at the low altitudes they had been flying over the target were slim.

What's more, the mass of enemy men and tanks would have also seen the parachute and would quickly converge on Spencer's position. They would also be looking for Stewart's plane.

Hopefully a combat search and rescue would find both men soon and bring them in safe and sound. It was reassuring to know a Harrier flight in their sister squadron would soon be flying over the target again to photograph the wrecked and burning mass of enemy vehicles that Shadow Flight had left behind.

But the sour feeling in Hartley's stomach only got worse as they approached the nearest Harrier hide. Something told him he would never see either man alive again.

The city of Bielefeld lay ahead of the three Harriers. Directed by air traffic to the urban hide, Hartley checked his maps and made sure to get the approach vectors right. If he didn't, his Harriers stood a good chance of being shot down by the Rapiers stationed around the hide's perimeter.

He steered his Harrier towards the center of the city and landed clumsily on top of the large three-story parking garage. The aircraft technicians hurriedly threw up a grey camouflage net above each Harrier as they landed.

Hartley wasn't a big fan of the urban hides. They

seemed more vulnerable to discovery compared to being tucked away in a forest and under the natural canopy of trees.

Hartley sat in the cockpit drenched in sweat. He knew they was supposed to bear losses, but this seemed too much to take. Bellamy, Stewart, and Spencer - nearly half of his flight gone in one day. He climbed out of the cockpit and descended the ladder to the bare concrete below.

Walking around his Harrier, Hartley was gob smacked at the extent of the damage. He stuck his fist through a hole that had been punched into the left horizontal stabilizer. The plane's underbelly had a few more large holes carved out of it. Chunks of the plane were simply missing. He felt lucky to be alive given the extent of the plane's damage.

He walked back around the front of the aircraft and spotted Davis climbing down from his cockpit.

The tall man's face was twisted into an expression of rage. He strode towards Hartley, his fists flexing and balling up. Less than half a meter away, he stopped. Davis towered over him. He sneered in disgust.

"Just what the bloody hell do you think you were doing out there?" he shouted. Hartley stepped back. Davis's anger was finally unbuttoned before him. They had had their differences over the years but nothing like this. Nelson saw what was happening and hurried out of his cockpit.

Davis threw his helmet to the pavement. "We were out there with no top cover and no suppression and you ordered the attack anyways! What were you thinking?"

Hartley put his hands on his hips, the anger welling up inside of him. "We did the mission we were ordered to do and --," he stammered.

Davis marched up to Hartley and grabbed him. "And what?" he shouted. The spittle landed on Hartley's face. "You could have turned us back any time. But you kept us going and now Stewart and Spencer are dead. You fucking murderer!"

Nelson was in between them now, pulling Davis away. Hartley's wingman tried to speak calmly to him. "It's over now," he said. "It's done, Davis. Let it go."

Davis took a step back then turned around suddenly and punched Hartley in the face. Hartley fell back towards the pavement, more out of shock than pain. Davis's fist had mostly caught Hartley's helmet on its way to his jaw.

Nelson pulled Davis back again. "Now you've done it, mate," he said to Davis. "That's a court martial you're looking at." Davis wiped his mouth with his sleeve and spat at the ground near Hartley.

"Put me under arrest then," said Davis. "I'll be happy to testify."

Hartley shook his head and stood up slowly. He rubbed his jaw. "Take a walk mate," he said calmly. "Sort yourself out. We'll talk later."

Davis looked at Hartley with a stunned wild expression. For a moment, he stood there speechless. "…Right" he finally said. "And then we'll see what you have to say for yourself." Nelson walked away with Davis.

Hartley pulled out a sweat-drenched cigarette from his flight suit and lit it. It tasted like a backed-up toilet, which suited exactly how he felt at that moment. He breathed out and watched the abandoned city streets from the top of the parking garage. Somewhere deep inside of him, he felt Davis had a point.

I could have called off the attack. I also could have left those Hinds to be dealt with by friendly ground fire. Was I reckless? Did I needlessly endanger the lives of my men? And what would have happened if that battalion had gotten through? How many on our side would have died then?

Despite his self-assurances, Hartley was shaken. The team of men he had carefully cultivated over the years was unraveling before his eyes on the very first day of the war.

How long could this go on before everything broke down completely?

6

Spencer plummeted to earth, tumbling as he plunged towards the trees. When the parachute finally opened a half-second later, he was jerked upwards. He turned and watched the destruction behind him on the highway for a moment.

When he was seven, he had been playing with matches and accidentally set the carpet on fire in the house. The flames quickly spread down the length of the hallway, consuming everything in its path. The smell and the chaos it had created were reminiscent of what he saw below but on a larger scale. Much larger.

The landscape in and around the strip of highway was a collection of burnt steel and bodies. Ungainly dark spots where the bomblets landed and exploded were everywhere. Some of the vehicles in the middle of the tank column tried to reverse, only to run backwards into the conflagration behind them. Others tried to go forward and found the same. Men rushed back and forth trying to find a way out of the hellscape.

HARRIER AIR WAR: 1985

Spencer felt a certain glee in knowing that he had been partly to blame for it all. In truth, he had never really been able to visualize what the bombs would look like when used against real targets in a real shooting war, despite having practiced countless times dropping the same weapon on groups of dummy targets. Now he knew the truth and it was better than he could have ever hoped for.

The ground came up towards him fast. Spencer hoped he wouldn't be impaled on a tree on the way down. The wind brought his parachute a few hundred meters west of where Stewart's plane had augured into a field and skidded several hundred meters into the woods.

Spencer felt for the 9mm Browning in his holster and pulled it out, chambering a round. He suddenly became aware of the whizzing sound of bullets passing near him. Above him, the canopy already had several holes in it.

To the south were several hundred men who were extremely angry at him. That wasn't anything new for Spencer, but it was the first time the aggrieved party was armed with heavy weapons.

The canopy of his parachute caught on a beech tree's limbs on the way down. Spencer's body miraculously missed getting stabbed by any sharp branches though he heard the back of his flight suit rip open from neck to waist.

By the time his descent stopped, he was suspended several meters above the ground with his legs and arms caught in a web-like array of tangled parachute lines. He swayed like a marionette thrown away by a bored child.

He knew the Russians would be coming for him very soon. If he wanted to escape capture or torture, he needed to act fast. He reached for the cutter near his leg and pulled it from its scabbard. Spencer worked the curved steel blade against the parachute lines, slicing himself free little by little. He worked fast, imagining the enemy getting closer and closer to him. If he took too long, he would meet the ground with a rifle shoved in his face.

The last line split apart and Spencer let out a surprised laugh as he dropped suddenly to the ground. A vehicle's engines rumbled somewhere to the south. Spencer took the safety off his pistol and ran north, zigzagging deeper into the forest. As he bounded over the uneven ground, his left foot caught on an upraised root.

He went sprawling and landed face down on a large stone with a loud metallic clunk. His helmet caught the impact and he felt clever for wearing it. But when he stood up to resume his sprint, he collapsed as soon as he put his weight on his right leg.

Spencer gritted his teeth and prayed. *Dear god, don't let it be broken.* He listened to the sound of men brushing through the dense foliage less than a dozen meters behind him. He tried once more to stand up, this time slowly.

With a tear in his eye, he shifted his weight back to his right leg. The pain shot up around his ankle but with some gritting of teeth, he was able to limp forward on it. Every few steps, he used a hand to steady himself on a tree trunk.

He continued further into the dense trees and bushes. The shouting behind him grew louder. From the variety of angry voices, Spencer estimated no more than four or five men. The odds weren't totally hopeless - just extremely bad. He rested against a tree trunk and grit his teeth against the sharp agony of what he presumed was a twisted ankle.

The initial shock of ejection and injury started wearing off. His thoughts became much clearer, more focused as he rested. *I'll never outrun them. Need to hide.*

Spencer looked around for anything that would conceal his body. He had been through the search and evasion training course at Mountbatten. He tried to tell himself this was no different. But it was.

The men out there wouldn't just rough him up if they found him. Surrender or not, they would interrogate him, beat him beyond recognition and - if he was lucky, they would kill him. Suddenly, the war was no longer a wonderful adventure. It was here and very real.

There was some shrubbery nearby that was nearly waist-height. Spencer took his map from his kneeboard and ripped off a generous chunk. He chewed on it and crumpled the rest of the torn map, which he shoved through the notch of the tree trunk where he rested.

He took two large strides and let himself fall into the shrubs. The thorns on the branches pricked into his skin. Spencer cursed his luck and wondered what else could go wrong.

The shouting of his pursuers grew louder. One of them yelled in garbled German to come out. Spencer curled up into a ball, trying to make himself as small and insignificant as he could. He dug into the soft ground and tried his hardest not to curse as the thorns stabbed him.

The footsteps came on. Spencer stopped digging and held the Browning to his chest. He waited and held his breath. The sound of his heart beating in his ears seemed deafening.

He squinted hard, hoping to keep the whites of his eyes from giving away his position. A single man waded through the tall grass towards where he lay. He wore dark green combat fatigues and a helmet.

The enemy soldier held an AK-47 with a bayonet affixed to the end. Spencer instantly knew he would never be taken alive. He tried hard not to think about the cold steel blade slicing through his organs. Should he stand up and fire while he still had an element of surprise? It wouldn't last long. The other men would be here within seconds once they heard the gunshot. He waited. The man stepped closer.

He kept his head to the ground and tensed. The man stepped towards him again. Two steps away. One step. Spencer tightened his grip on the pistol.

A gunshot rang out in the distance.

The man swivelled right and then sprinted through the foliage and disappeared into the trees. Spencer let out a long slow breath. The pounding of his heart eased a little. Then he heard another set of boots tromping through the bush at high speed. He stayed in a foetal position and closed his eyes tight.

He felt a kick in the gut and heard a surprised yelp. Spencer struggled to breathe and then slowly got up. An enemy soldier lay sprawled in the thicket less than a meter away. He was face down and his rifle had fallen out of his hands, clattering noisily on the forest floor. As he struggled to get up, Spencer raised his pistol. His hands shook.

His finger caressed the trigger. The man groaned. If he shot now, he would announce his presence to more men.

He couldn't run. There was only one thing left to do.

Spencer fell on top of the man's back and wrapped his arms around the Russian's neck. As he squeezed, the man wiggled back and forth. Spencer held on as if he were a drowning man clutching a life preserver.

The Russian's hand shot out towards his rifle. Spencer used his body to angle the man away from it. He was surprised at how much energy it took to simply keep the man in place and maintain his hold on him. The energy drained from his body as he took big gulps of air.

Remembering the blade he kept near his boot for cutting the parachute cords, he plunged one hand down to pull it out while holding the Russian's throat back in his other arm. The enemy soldier was wiggling out of the hold slowly but surely. Spencer felt the grip of the knife in his hand and brought it up high.

With all his remaining strength, he pulled the Russian backwards and drove the knife down. The blade dug into the man's soft flesh. Spencer's stomach churned when he pulled out the knife and heard a gurgling noise.

An arc of dark red blood sprayed up into the air. The Russian let out a low angry sound. Spencer plunged the knife into the man's neck once again. The big man crawled away, clutching at his throat. He let out a long series of gasps and then suddenly stopped, his eyes open towards the blue sky.

Spencer sat on the ground, exhausted. He wanted nothing more than to lay down and rest. But he knew he needed to get out of here fast.

It wasn't just the danger of being discovered. It was the

fact of what he had done. His stomach heaved and he threw up. Immediately, he felt a little better. He put the knife away and took the Russian's assault rifle. With some effort, he managed to stand up, using the butt of the weapon for support.

Spencer looked down at the Russian, who was clearly dead. Another shot rang out to the east.

He staggered west.

7

The late morning light filtered in through open spaces along the third floor of the parking garage. Less than 24 hours ago, the structure had been an unassuming building that gave downtown Bielefeld citizens a place for their cars while they shopped in the nearby supermarket. Now it was in the process of being converted to a Harrier hide.

The smell of dirty engine oil wafted through the air. Drawers full of spare parts and tools were brought down from the back of large flatbed trucks. Technicians hurried back and forth as the supply trucks arrived. Behind them were the boxy vehicles that served as mobile command centers for the squadron.

Hartley took some comfort in seeing that Briscoe's vehicle was among them. He had always liked the man professionally. He was a rare breed of operations officers - unassuming, flexible, and willing to listen to the pilots.

Hartley wondered if he should say something about Davis then put the thought out of his mind. He couldn't afford to lose another pilot and he was willing to bet there were deeper issues at work here. Other men in the squadron had warned him that Davis was damaged goods after his accident. Hartley had given the man a chance, though, and he had proved a capable pilot.

Nelson sat across from Hartley on the hood of a family sedan. They were in the middle of a game of chess using a cheap little plastic travel set they had found in the back seat. Hartley moved his black queen to Nelson's edge of the board and fumbled to remove the white rook from the hole in which it was pegged.

"Check," Hartley announced.

Nelson shook his head at the mate. "Well played," he said.

Hartley looked towards the ramp with a blank expression. Nelson coughed. "Nice game," he said. "I should have watched that queen slowly edging its way up the side of the board. It's always the slow knife that kills, isn't it?"

"What? Oh...right," said Hartley. He felt as if he were about to burst. Dunhill and Martin had still not arrived and no one seemed to know where they were. Was he doomed to lose everybody today? How could he have prevented it? The right choices were out there somewhere. But how could he recognize them?

"Nelson...I need to know something," Hartley said. "Do you blame me for what happened out there? I mean...Stewart and Spencer."

Nelson didn't look up from putting the chess pieces back in their peg holes on the little plastic board.

"I won't second guess you for making a call out there," he said. "You needed to make some kind of decision and you did. That's what flight leaders do."

Hartley shook his head. *Hardly a ringing endorsement.*

"Yes, I understand that," Hartley said. There was a long silence. "Would you have made the same decision?"

Nelson put Hartley's black bishop back to its starting position on the board. "If everyone had come back safe would you still be asking yourself that question? Would we be having this conversation right now?"

Hartley knew the answer was no. "Well, that's not the point, is it? I mean --."

Nelson put a hand up to interrupt him. "That is precisely the point," he said. "You're the one who has to live with it - not Davis, not me. Judging by hindsight is easy enough when you're not culpable for the results. We stopped an enemy battalion of tanks from reaching the front at the cost of two pilots. What would those men in the 1st Armored Division have thought?"

Hartley got up from his chair. "I just bloody well wish Davis would think of that," he said.

Nelson closed the lid on the chess game and put it back in his bag. "I'll go talk to him," he said.

"Tell him to be ready. We're going up again soon," he said. Hartley walked to the hide's ops command vehicle, sensing that there was something already waiting.

Inside the large box-bodied vehicle were several men and women busily talking on the radio, marking positions on maps in grease pencil.

Briscoe murmured into a radio headset. He didn't look up as Hartley approached. "Looks like we're getting pushed back around Hannover," he said. "Belgians are pulling west from Springe."

Hartley nodded. "Looks bad."

Briscoe kept his eyes down on the map and took a sip of tea. "Isn't it," he said.

Hartley sensed he should get to the point right away, but Briscoe seemed to know already what he wanted.

"Your butty's still not out of the fire yet," he said, referring to Spencer and Stewart. "There's a search and rescue operation being organized but the area's still pretty hot."

"If there's any way we can get in on the operation, I want out there," said Hartley.

Briscoe dropped his pencil and looked up at him. "Waste of a Harrier right now," he said. "Top cover? Get a fighter. Suppression? Get an attack helicopter. Face it, man. There are better suited men and planes for that. There's other trouble afoot right now for you."

Hartley knew Briscoe had a point. "Well, what is happening then?"

Briscoe brought out a large map of the Lower Saxony area. The little blue dotted marks showed NATO frontline forces snaked along the Weser River to the north. It looked like Hamburg had already been captured. Bremerhaven and Bremen were still in NATO hands but dangerously close to the front lines. South of Bremen, the dotted marks jutted out towards the east, rounding out near Hannover.

Hartley looked at all the little red dots that showed the Warsaw Pact's axis of attack in the sector. There was so much red and so little blue on the map. Hartley couldn't believe they were holding on to any ground at all.

"As I mentioned before, there's a fighting withdrawal happening near Hannover. The 33rd Armored Brigade shifted south a few kilometers to help keep the Belgians in the game. That's left a gap in the lines with the 11th Brigade.

"Word from above is that Ivan's caught on and is trying to thread the needle with a tank division. They're trying to take advantage of the situation," said Briscoe. "If they manage to work their way around into the rear, our defenses around Hannover will certainly collapse very quickly. The Russians will be over the Weser before nightfall."

Briscoe pulled out a sheaf of papers with a list of operational Harriers on it. Hartley's name was near the top. Spencer, Stewart, and Bellamy's names were crossed out. The other two flights in the squadron had about half their names crossed out too. It was awful to look at.

"An entire division," said Hartley in shock. "We should be out there right now, shouldn't we?"

"Soon anyways. We could hit them now, but they're dispersed too widely to destroy completely. That would require more aircraft than we currently have available. We need to funnel them into an area and get them to bunch up.

We're deploying ground forces right now in such a way as to lead them exactly where we want them."

Hartley stared at the photos of enemy tanks and infantry fighting vehicles that had been taken by the Number 4 Squadron Harriers.

Briscoe pointed to the map. "We have some West German mechanized infantry deploying to the northwest of Hildesheim. As the Soviet division moves in, they'll come under harassing fire from the Milan-mounted Marders concealed in the forests dotted around these fields.

To the south of the town, we'll have artillery-delivered minefields deploy just as Ivan arrives in the area. The only way forward for them will be to go through Hildesheim. After that, Ivan's recon units will find the way clear all the way to Diekholzen."

"Never heard of it," said Hartley.

Briscoe nodded. "Neither had I until thirty minutes ago. The Russians won't pass up the chance to go for it, especially since the highway they'll be on bridges the Innerste River.

Once they get through, the shortest way west is down the L485 and towards Diekholzen. It's a small town in this deep narrow valley. The division commander will need to bunch up his forces to get them through as quickly as possible. With harassing fire from artillery, he'll be in a big rush."

Hartley nodded. "And that's where we'll get them," he said with a grin.

Briscoe took a sip of tea. "Looks that way, doesn't it? The L485 isn't a very big highway. The hills on either side will force them to bunch together as they pass through towards the town. If you can time it right, they'll be in for a proper pasting."

Hartley nodded in approval, looking over the map. Beside it were Briscoe's notes on the attack procedure. It would start with an artillery bombardment once the division was nearly through the valley. The bombardment was designed to create maximum confusion.

After that would come the anti-tank helicopters to hit at the air defenses and then finally all the Harriers from Number 3 and Number 4 Squadrons would destroy the tanks and infantry carriers. Hartley loved the plan. Each phase built upon the other until it reached a terrifying crescendo of destruction.

"How many Harriers are left?" he asked, bracing himself for the answer.

Briscoe ran down the list and shrugged. "With the most recent losses, it's down to twenty-three," he said. "Still an impressive amount of ordnance to drop on them."

Hartley got up from his seat and walked out of the tent. Now that he had a mission to perform with the men, he was worried about Davis. He could ground the man for throwing a punch at him, even throw him in a stockade until he saw the light of reason. But there was work to do.

Hartley walked down the ramp towards the second floor of the parking garage. Davis sat on the hood of a Volkswagen, smoking a cigarette and looking out over the shops and stores of the Bielefeld city center.

British I Corps was headquartered here only a few days ago but had now moved out into the field to do its job. Since a few half-hearted attempts at bombing the town this morning, the Russians had largely left the place alone. Still, the eastern section of the city had come under artillery fire less than an hour ago and the deserted Catterick Barracks there had been levelled by a few lucky hits.

Black smoke curled up from the southeast. The nearby loudspeakers kept blaring in German to no one, telling the long-since departed residents to evacuate. Davis didn't turn his head as Hartley approached.

"Something big is in the air," said Hartley. He sat down on the hood of the Volkswagen and lit a smoke. It tasted awful.

Davis turned towards him, his face flashing from surprise to anger. He stared at Hartley and then at the ground. "Yeah?" he said quietly.

"Armored division south of Hannover," said Hartley. "They're pulling out all the stops for it. Artillery, helos, and the both Harrier squadrons. I won't lie - I'll need you up there with us."

Davis took a drag of his cigarette and nodded. "What's the word on Spence and Stu?" he asked. Hartley was taken aback. He had never heard Davis use their nicknames before in all the years they'd worked together.

"No word back yet but they're trying their best," said Hartley.

Davis stubbed the cigarette out on the hood of the abandoned vehicle and threw the butt to the concrete ground. "Listen...about before," he said. "About what happened before, I'm sorry. It's just so bloody...where was the artillery?"

Hartley tossed his own cigarette out and shrugged. "I don't know," he said. "We'll never really know what happened back there. I have a feeling this thing's going to get much messier before it gets cleaner. We need to be ready for it, mate."

Hartley slid off the hood and didn't look back. He could hear Davis sniffling. "Look, Davis. Clean yourself up a bit and come up in five minutes for the briefing," he said. "And next time if you have problems with my decisions, bring them up privately."

He walked up to the next level of the parking garage and met Nelson, who sat in the back of a van with the hatch open. He was reading a paperback novel. Hartley tapped the open pages. "Time to shine," he said. "Waiting for you in the tent. Be there in five."

Nelson tossed the book behind him. "What about Davis?" he asked.

Hartley nodded. "He'll be there too."

8

Spencer heard the low whooping sound of the helicopter's large rotors. Having been at Gutersloh for two years, he instantly recognized the sound of the Puma helicopters. They were here for him and Stewart. Soon they would be back on board and flying towards friendly lines. The nightmare he had been living through for the past hour was nearly over.

He turned on his personal locator beacon and hoped the helicopter would triangulate his position faster than the enemy. The remains of an entire tank battalion were less than a kilometer south of where he lay hiding in the thick brush of the forest. So far, he had been lucky enough to evade the men who were searching for him, but he knew it wouldn't last forever.

Thirty minutes ago, the gunshots in the distance had stopped completely. The enemy search party had returned about five minutes ago. Their loud angry shouts indicated they had finally found the body of the enemy soldier that Spencer had killed.

Since the enemy had left in the direction of the gunshots and returned, he had had nearly twenty minutes to limp further north from the body's location.

Less than a hundred yards from a tree line that opened into a flat open field, Spencer had hidden himself well in an area thick with vegetation. He had covered himself in moss and twigs and leaves and burrowed into the bush after laying thick leafy branches on the ground to help cover his hide.

It wasn't perfect, but it would have to do. The ants crawled over his body, making him itch. Spencer kept movement to a bare minimum but the feel of the bugs wandering up and down his bare skin was beginning to drive him crazy. He hoped that the Puma would land soon and take him away from this place.

The helicopter came towards his position at tree top level. Somewhere to the south came the metallic clang of anti-aircraft artillery. Spencer worried that the Puma would be shot down before it had a chance to pick him up. The enemy flak was very much active and firing at his rescuers.

Just when he expected the helo to settle down in the field beyond the tree line, he heard its rotors whine and turn back. The helicopter circled around and passed over him, continuing towards the south.

Spencer checked his beacon to make sure it was active. The green knob was turned to the Distress Channel setting. He wanted to talk into it or listen to the aircrew above him, but he dared not do it yet.

Next pass. I'll get them on the next pass over.

But the sound of the helo remained far to the south.

Spencer gritted his teeth in frustration as the sound lingered on the other side of the highway. *Look here, you silly bastards. You're on the wrong side of the road!*

Spencer checked again that his beacon was working properly. He dared to push the green button on the side of the device that let him listen to the aircrew, just to make sure the device was working.

"Brother Two in position, await--." The voice on the other end was loud and clear.

The leaves crunched and a twig snapped. Spencer let go of the button and closed his eyes. He knew he was caught. There was nothing to do but wait. He held his Browning tight to his chest and waited with his finger on the trigger.

To his left, there was the sound of another step being taken in his direction. The enemy approached. Spencer thought about killing himself to avoid interrogation and torture. But he knew that wasn't the right away. Not after all this.

He would wait until he was discovered and then shoot the man in the face. After that, he would take his chances. If he was going to die, he wasn't going to make it easy for them.

The Puma circled far off in the distance. The crackling sound of the enemy guns grew to a steady hiss. Spencer wondered if the men in the helicopter wouldn't be joining him down here very soon in the mud and misery and ants.

He gritted his teeth and waited. The enemy was closing in on his position from the left. He was less than two feet away from where he lay. He brought the barrel of the pistol up and waited.

Suddenly, the branch on top of him shifted and he saw daylight. A figure stood above him. The barrel of the rifle he held stared at him in the face - a cold black tunnel about to take his life. Spencer aimed his pistol up and tried to pull the trigger. The man's boot came down hard on the inside of his wrist.

His hand and forearm slammed down to the ground and the pistol rattled out of his grip. Spencer looked up into the barrel of a rifle mere inches from his face.

He closed his eyes and waited for the end. A few regrets fluttered through his mind. Setting fire to the mess hall piano that one time was among them. Then the moment passed and he was at peace with his life.

"Do it," he murmured. "Just go ahead and do it, you bastard."

The man looked like an incarnation of death. He wore a dark blue beret and his face was painted black and he wore a scowl as he stared down at Spencer.

"You can do it to yourself if you want," he said through a thick Scouse accent. "But I thought you might want a lift back with us instead. I'm Jones. I'm here with the recce team to pull you out of here."

Spencer felt the confusion wash over him and then smiled, extending a hand. Jones took his hand and lifted Spencer up off the ground. "Are you sound enough to walk?" he asked, noticing Spencer favoring his left leg.

He shook his head. "I twisted my bloody ankle. How far is it to the helicopter?"

"No helicopter right now," Jones said. "We're driving you a ways from here for pickup at a safer location. Can you walk? If not, I'm afraid I have some bad news for you."

Spencer hopped forwards towards the clearing. He felt the pain shooting up in his leg again. This time it was even more painful than before. The adrenaline had stopped compensating for the injury. He also suspected his ankle was swollen. The soles of his boots dug into the swollen ankle as he took each painful step.

"What about that Puma? They were looking for me on the wrong bloody side of the road!" said Spencer.

Spencer clung onto Jones. The first step was searing hot agony. They stopped.

"You had about a platoon worth of men on this side of the road searching for you and your mate," said Jones. "The Puma distracted them. Drew them off your scent."

They made their way to the clearing. Jones pulled out a handheld radio and adjusted the frequency. "Fox Green, this is Fox Charlie, I have the package. Condition is damaged but mobile. Over."

Jones scanned the open field in front of him with a pair of binoculars. Spencer rested in a crouch, putting his weight on his uninjured foot.

Ten seconds later, the radio chirped out a reply. "Roger that, Fox Charlie. We have a visual. You are clear to go. Say again, you are clear."

Jones stood up. "Lean on me," he said. "I know it might hurt but we've got to move fast. There are still enemies around here."

Spencer nodded and wrapped his right arm around Jones' neck. The recce team member jogged across the open field towards a clump of trees about three hundred meters away.

Spencer felt the pain surging through his body with each agonizing step. He nearly stopped at one point, but he knew there was a good chance he'd be left behind if he did.

"Come on, man!" said Jones as he pulled him onwards. "Let's get out of here!"

The uneven ground was hell on Spencer's twisted ankle. He stumbled and pitched himself forward, nearly bringing Jones down with him. The last fifty meters of the run were a blur. The pain shot up his leg, as Jones cursed at him. Each step was a howling agony as he stumbled and fumbled onwards.

Finally, it ended. Jones shoved Spencer through the copse of beech trees. The Land Rover was so well-hidden by the shrubs and branches that Spencer had not even recognized it until he was within arm's reach. Three men stood around the Land Rover, one of them with a sniper's rifle. Another man talked on comms and the other man was behind the wheel.

Jones pointed Spencer to the back of the Land Rover. He climbed in and sat down, letting the waves of anguish wash over him. He was in too much agony to feel relieved or even thankful for his rescue.

Without warning, the Land Rover started up and the bumpy ride began. The vehicle jolted forward over the field, heading north towards a gentle sloping hill covered in trees. Spencer felt the pain in his ankle as the Land Rover lurched and jolted over the rocks and bumps. Jones and another man in the unit sat beside him, swaying back and forth.

The Land Rover drove into a thick forest. The branches of the trees scraped at Jones as the little vehicle sped around the trees. The forest was dense and Spencer didn't think a vehicle could ever fit in here, never mind be driven through it.

The Land Rover halted in a forest clearing. The men in front jumped out and started spreading camouflage netting around the vehicle. Jones put out a hand for Spencer who took it, sliding slowly out of the back of the little truck. The other three men brought all the equipment out of the back except for a long bag in the middle of the Land Rover's bed.

Spencer leaned against the back of the Land Rover and pointed to it. "What's that bit of kit?" he asked.

Jones cleared his throat. "That's Warrant Officer Stewart," he said. He walked away into the center of the clearing.

Spencer looked down at the body bag and cried.

9

Dunhill and Martin pulled up into the parking garage in a small civilian truck. Hartley knew better than to ask where they had gotten it.

"Nice of you gentlemen to join us," he said. Both men clambered out the back of the vehicles and retrieved their bags from the back. "Hope the war didn't inconvenience you too much."

They walked up towards the top of the garage together with Davis and Nelson. Hartley tried to hide his relief at the arrival of the two replacement pilots. Although both men were relatively new to flying Harriers, they had been through the training at Wittering six months ago and were combat-qualified.

"Puma broke down on the way here," said Dunhill. "Wandered around in the dark for two hours and then found a farm with a truck just sitting there with the keys still in it." He snapped his fingers. "We drove to your last hide, but you were already gone. Been playing silly buggers all 'til now."

Hartley looked over at Martin, who was unusually quiet. The young man was clearly shaken from the ordeal. As the two extra pilots in the flight, they were expected to fill in for casualties and now here they were. Hartley couldn't believe how quickly things were happening. *We've got to fly more carefully. No more John Wayne out there.*

"Get your kit on and suit up," said Hartley. "We'll go over the mission details in the cockpit. There just isn't much time left for a proper sit-down briefing right now."

Five minutes later, Hartley was walking around his Harrier. There were still a few holes punched into the airframe, but the technician informed him that the avionics were repaired. An elevator had been replaced.

The BLU 755 cluster bombs were on his hardpoints and he checked that the big black cluster bombs were properly attached to the plane. Inside the cramped cockpit, the warning lights were dark.

He entered the mission waypoints on the navigation system. The map showing him the target coordinates displayed on the circular screen directly in front of him. The plan was to fly south and meet up with the rest of the Harriers in No. 3 and No. 4 squadron and wait for the Belgian F-16 escorts to arrive.

Hartley smiled. He had worked with the Belgians before and enjoyed the professionalism of the pilots. They didn't have the greatest equipment to work with, but they did their very best with what they had.

He watched Davis climb into the cockpit of the Harrier across from him. Davis settled down inside and looked over at Hartley, giving him a thumbs up. Hartley hesitated and did the same. The ground crew had built a very rough makeshift ramp on the top of the garage.

Hartley wheeled the Harrier towards it and punched the throttle and nozzle level forward. The Harrier sped down the ramp and pitched up the sharp incline at the end of it. The plane leapt upwards into the skies over downtown Bielefeld. He had no doubt that for Davis, it would bring back memories of flying off the ski jump on the *HMS Hermes* three years earlier in the South Atlantic.

Hartley breathed a sigh of relief. It was good to be back in the air, away from the problems of the ground. He worked the Harrier into a roll and checked how the aircraft responded to his input. The plane snapped back as he brought the flight stick left. It was his old plane again. The ground crew had worked their usual miracles. It amazed him every time.

Once the five Harriers were in the air, Hartley went over the briefing with them once again for the benefit of Dunhill and Martin. The city dropped away below them and they headed southwest.

"This is a complex mission with lots of moving parts," said Hartley. "Don't be surprised if things don't go off as planned. I want you to be alert and flexible enough to adapt to any changes but don't try to be a hero. Better to come back to base for another try than to get shot down for nothing."

Hartley wondered if he was talking to the other pilots or to himself. He shrugged. It didn't matter.

As they passed back towards Gutersloh, Hartley couldn't help but look out to his left side to see the base. It was almost destroyed. The long runway had a large dark hole near the middle. Several of the hangars were damaged. A few of the older buildings on the base were simply gone. He felt a tinge of sadness and then forced himself to look away.

The other Harriers came into view, flying low and fast near the treetops. They were a mere dot at first on the horizon. Impossible to make out if you were too high above them or if you weren't really looking. Hartley smiled, glad to have the other two flights join him. He said nothing as he noticed the other Harriers line up into formation with Shadow Flight.

"Good morning," Hartley said calmly into radio. "Nice to see you all."

"Talon Flight checking in," he heard. The three Harriers circled around low and got behind Shadow Flight in a wedge formation. The pair of Harriers in Archer Flight approached low and got on the other side of the wedge.

The earlier telebriefing had given them all the details they needed. Planning between the flights had been conducted to consider the timing down to an exact second.

The other aircraft and helicopters in the strike would already be nearing the target to the south. Hartley hoped the artillery would come in this time. If not, they would be facing another difficult situation.

The squadron swept southwards. Hannover lay to the left. The great black and grey clouds of smoke poured up from the front lines and into the sky. The F-16s came into view far overhead. Hartley spoke to them. "Good morning, Matrix. Nice to see you."

"We're reading you loud and clear," came their response. Hartley smiled. *Professional. To the point.*

Hartley noticed that much of the eastern edge of the city was ablaze. He hadn't heard any up-to-date information on how the battle was going, but it looked like NATO was losing ground.

In the grand scheme of things, the destruction of the Russian tank battalion had been a drop in the bucket. There were always more out there - a second echelon, a third echelon. Wave after wave of Warsaw Pact forces were waiting to take up the fight when the previous onslaught of men and machines were no longer effective.

The flight kept low over the fields. The occasional low hill rose up from the plains. Hartley and the rest of the pilots kept their aircraft going fast and hugged the terrain as tightly as they could. The radar warning receiver near the HUD lit up, signalling search radar ahead. Hartley checked his watch and glanced at the map on his TACAN navigation screen. It was almost time.

He listened over the radio net, waiting intently for the signal to go. To the east, the Russian division was pouring through the valley that held the small West German town of Diekholzen. As he circled low and fast, Hartley watched as the smoking trail of Milan anti-tank missiles lashed out to hit the Russian tanks and men from nearly two kilometers away.

There were little flashes and puffs of smoke amid the hapless Russian armored division's lead elements. The main body of the division was herded further into the valley, trying to get its exposed flank tucked in beyond the range of the missiles.

Hartley listened to the forward air controller. "Good hits on the lead elements. They're really bunching up now! Fire mission, proceed."

The artillery slammed into the ground, sending plumes of black and brown earth and dust spraying upwards. The barrage swept over the division all at once, catching the tanks and vehicles in the valley. The greatest effort was on the perimeter of the division, with the intent of preventing the regiments from dispersing or trying to make a run for it.

Hartley knew the ground commander would have realized by now they were in a trap. Some of the vehicles would try to get out of the kill box. Chieftains lay to the Soviet division's rear, firing at them from range, herding the Soviets onward into the kill box. The fire poured down on them again and again like sheets of rain.

When the artillery finally lifted, the Cobras and Apaches flew up on either side of the valley behind the protective terrain of the mountains.

The helicopters popped up and fired off their Hellfire anti-tank missiles. The lead vehicles were hit along with the command vehicles. Hartley listened to a pair of Apache pilots yell excitedly as they scored hit after hit on the mobile AAA and SAM vehicles.

It was nearly showtime and all had gone well enough so far. A mayday call went out over the net. One of the Cobras had taken an unlucky hit from a handheld SAM. Hartley tried to scan the hills for where it might be. A telltale flash on the southern slope of a nearby hill gave it away.

"They're going north!" he heard from the forward air controller. The tanks below were making a rapid and unexpected thrust towards the open fields.

No one had expected the Russian commanders to orchestrate such a maneuver amid all the death and destruction. Hartley shook his head. If they managed to break out of the valley, there might be enough of them left to hit the NATO rear very badly.

Hartley checked his watch. It was time. The Harriers screamed over the hill at low level. The columns of smoke and dust made it hard to see much of anything. A burst of AAA leapt up and Hartley felt his plane jolt upwards for a moment.

The HUD went blank. Leaning forward to the bombsight next to the HUD, he watched with one eye on a red dot while the other eye looked out the front of the plane. When the red dot on the sight appeared just over the green and brown mass of men and machines below, he flicked up the bomb cover and pickled the cluster bombs.

Hartley shoved the flight stick right. The Harrier immediately started to roll hard left.

Hartley stood on the right rudder. The Harrier was back under his control, but he needed to focus hard to keep it that way. A few seconds later, Davis came over the radio. "Sunshine to Shadow, your ordnance is stuck on your left wing."

Hartley felt the Harrier roll again. He looked over his shoulder. Sure enough, the cluster bombs sat there stubbornly on the hardpoint, clinging for dear life. Hartley adjusted the trim and throttled up.

Behind him, two motorized rifle regiments were obliterated. The dark cloud of smoke billowed up over the flaming wreckage of armored vehicles. In an instant, the lush green and peaceful valley below had turned into a cauldron of flaming death.

The bomblets had cut a wide swath of destruction over the main body of the division. What had been a carefully assembled and trained military force only moments before was now a heap of smoldering wreckage. The bodies inside the vehicles would not even be recognizable to their own mothers.

Number 4 squadron came next with its attack run, followed almost immediately by its reconnaissance Harriers.

Hartley didn't need to see the film to know what was happening. The secondary explosions of fuel and ammunition were loud enough to hear over the roar of his engine. He glanced over his shoulder again at the black bulbous-shaped bomb stuck to his wing and cursed to himself.

The radar warning receiver shrieked in his ears. Turning back, he saw an air search radar indication. One of the men from Number 4 shouted over the radio. "Missile launch! I've got a missile launch!"

Hartley watched the snaking trail of an air-to-air missile close in fast on the Harrier. The pilot had barely enough time to drop flare and bank left. Too late. The missile exploded only a few meters away from the Harrier and the aircraft puffed out in a ball of fire and shrapnel.

"Where the hell is our top cover?" demanded Hartley. No one answered. Were they shot down? On a lunch break? Picking up local girls? He felt the beads of sweat slide down his face.

"This is Shadow Three One, abort," Hartley said. "I say again, abort mission."

Below him, he saw the triangular forms of a pair of MiG-21s pass between him and the rest of Number 4 squadron's Harriers.

Hartley thought about the pair of AiM-9s on his hardpoints and felt grateful for packing them. He wasn't much of a match for a Mach-capable jet like the MiG-21 but he would be damned if he didn't try and fend them off. He dipped the Harrier's nose down.

Davis's voice blared over the radio. "I have a pair of twenty ones here at angels one, heading two two zero, turning back in towards us! No response from air cover!"

Hartley cleared his throat. "Shadow to Sunshine, get clear from here and return to base."

He glanced at the mirror to see Nelson behind him and to his left. Nelson hadn't any air-to-air missiles, but he was decent with the cannons and that was good enough.

Hartley turned sharp and brought the aircraft back over the fiery remains of the bombed-out vehicles. The flak reached up towards him. The tracers lashed out at his plane.

The MiGs flew straight towards him at high speed. First, they were simply a dot on the horizon and the next second, they filled his view. Nelson and Hartley fired their cannons at the enemy aircraft at close range. Both missed.

Both enemy fighters split off from one another as they shot past the Harriers. Hartley watched in his mirror as one plane went left and the other right, no doubt coming around quickly for a close-range missile kill.

Hartley smiled and tilted the nozzles of the Harrier towards the ground and pulled back the throttle lever. The aircraft slowed to a near hover and drifted upwards. He snapped the Harrier to the left and watched the MiG-21 come back around towards him.

As it arced in a tight right turn, he was certain the enemy pilot would be shocked to find the Harrier positioned far behind where it should have been. He almost felt sorry for the man. If Hartley had been flying a normal jet, he would have indeed been right at the MiG's 12 o'clock. Instead, he sat hovering on the inside of the MiG's turn.

Once the MiG passed him, Hartley opened up the throttle and pointed the nozzles behind him. He followed the MiG-21 on its turn. The Harrier was much slower, but it didn't matter. The Sidewinders locked on to their target. Hartley fired both missiles. "Fox Two!" he shouted.

The MiG tried to out turn the missiles and managed to avoid the first. The second missile chased the MiG as it tried to climb and exploded just short of the enemy plane. The MiG tumbled to the ground in a yellow and black ball of smoke and fire.

The white silk of a parachute appeared, floating above the wrecked Soviet division. Hartley didn't envy the man, who was about to land in a sea of fire and wreckage.

"Splash one MiG!" Hartley shouted.

Hartley turned to see where the other MiG had gone. It was a dot on the horizon, getting smaller with each passing second. The remaining Harriers of the squadrons were already headed for their dispersal areas.

Hartley gave a thumbs up to Nelson and they too turned northwest. He felt relieved to be leaving the area. The F-16s that had supposedly been flying top cover were still nowhere to be seen and were not responding on the radio. Hartley shrugged, knowing he would probably never find out what happened to them.

The flight back to Bielefeld was quiet enough. About ten minutes into the return flight, Nelson noticed it. "You're leaking fuel," he said.

Hartley groaned. The fuel warning was lit. Looking back, he noticed the black trail of fluid pouring out the back of the Harrier.

"More of a fuel dump than a leak," Hartley told Nelson.

He checked his gauge and estimated the time needed to get back to base.

"Looks like I'll barely make it," said Hartley. He thought about the cluster bomb still sitting dangerously on his hardpoint.

Nelson said nothing. Hartley distracted himself by listening to the chatter as the other four Harriers landed in Bielefeld. It was a relief that everybody in Shadow Flight had survived. The other flights in Number 3 squadron had made it back without any losses either.

Number 4 squadron had lost two Harriers, one from

the engagement with the MiG and the other from a shoulder-launched SAM. Still, it wasn't too bad for a day's work. Two entire regiments had been destroyed completely and a third would likely be held in check by mines and anti-tank missile fire. The trap had worked.

Three minutes out from Bielefeld, Hartley heard the first call over the radio net.

"Where the bloody hell did those come from?" shouted Davis. "How the hell did they get through?"

Another voice shouted out. "Disperse! Disperse! Get out of here as fast as you can!"

A rush of confused voices spilled out onto his channel. Hartley struggled to keep pace with them, trying to understand what was happening. "Shadow to Shadow Flight, come in. Tell me what's happening out there."

"We're being overrun!" he heard back. It was Dunhill. "We're dispersing!"

Hartley still wasn't sure what he was hearing. He stayed on the channel, trying to raise anyone else, asking for more details. Finally, he realized he was doing more harm than good. He kept quiet and listened as the Harriers took off and left the hide atop the parking garage in Bielefeld.

A minute later, Hartley had them in view. Dozens of Soviet helicopters dashed over the low buildings.

"Do you see that?" he asked Nelson.

"I see it. But I don't bloody believe it."

The other four Harriers flew low and fast in the

opposite direction. Hartley knew they would be low on fuel and ammunition. Although it ached to see them leave the hide without a fight, they were doing the right thing.

"Let's turn and go with them," said Hartley. He looked at his fuel situation knowing it would be tight no matter where they were going.

Nelson keyed his microphone twice to acknowledge.

Hartley was about to turn the Harrier around when he saw a trail of smoke go up from the city and strike one of the helos. The big Hind whirled around madly and lost altitude before disappearing into the cluttered streets below.

"You've got to be kidding me," he said. "We still have people there?"

Hartley sighed and kept the Harrier going straight towards the parking garage. The Russian helos buzzed past it. Some of them descended near the roof of the garage. Hartley brought the Harrier to full throttle, trying hard not to think about the precious fuel that was dwindling fast.

"Horatio, you go on with the others," he told Nelson. "That's an order."

He glanced in his rear-view mirror, watching Nelson turn away. Hartley was relieved that his wingman didn't fight him over it. He appreciated that about Nelson. He could always count on him to obey a direct order without a fuss.

He brought the Harrier high over the city, hoping there wouldn't be any serious air cover that would shoot him down instantly. Hartley spotted the Hinds circling the parking garage below. Several other Russian transport helicopters had landed on the rooftops of other buildings near downtown and some were visible to the southeast.

Hartley realized he was witnessing an airborne operation being carried out. Although the Russians probably weren't expending all that manpower just to take out a single Harrier hide, it seemed they already knew its location and were addressing the problem while seizing control of the city.

On his first pass, he slowed down just enough to see the tracers fly back and forth on the roof of the garage. He turned the Harrier in a sharp bank, listening to the fuel warning in his ear. He knew it was more stupid than courageous but as long as there were British soldiers down there, he would try to help them.

Hartley swung the Harrier around and brought it to a near-hover. He brought the plane towards the parking garage at 120 knots and kept the nozzles at seventy five percent angle. The big gray building filled his view. A Hind sat on the roof, its passengers disgorged from its belly. As he approached, the small arms fire knocked against his plane.

Two hundred yards away from the helicopter, he squeezed the trigger. The twin cannons rattled out from the Harrier and cut into the Hind. The tracers arced wildly across the rooftop.

The Hind was physically pushed over from the impact of the rounds. It tumbled over and over and lurched past the lip of the garage roof before falling to the street below on the other side. Hartley opened the throttle and flew past the former Harrier hide at high speed.

"This is Shadow, do I have anyone on this channel?" he said into his radio. All of the personnel and vehicles should be speeding away from the garage as fast as possible. Whoever was trapped there would have to take their chances with the Russians.

A faint voice came over the radio as Hartley's Harrier jet flew south.

"We're pulling out now with the last of the personnel," he heard. "We're the last ones leaving the garage now."

Hartley pulled the Harrier back in a tight turn. A pair of Hinds swept past the nose of his plane, traveling west. He had to resist the urge to chase them and shoot them down. It would have been so easy.

He brought the Harrier to slow speed and headed at streetlight level down the wide city road that led towards the garage. He peered through his empty HUD and tried to spot it. At last a tan vehicle emerged from the front of the parking garage and turned south.

"I have a visual on you," said Hartley. "I'll try to help you get out of here. Just drive like hell!"

Hartley watched the little Unimog veer around the abandoned civilian vehicles in the road. He made a tight turn as he approached the intersection where the truck went. The left wing groaned slightly as it bumped against a bank's sign. "Because you deserve the best," it proclaimed in German.

As it passed south towards Autobahn 2, Hartley swore at the man behind the wheel for driving like his grandma on the way back from Brighton. He shook his head and kept the plane at a near-hover, hoping to escape the notice of the aircraft buzzing above them.

He brought the plane down the street towards the next intersection. The nose of his Harrier poked past the department store on his right. The Hind came straight for him. It was less than a hundred yards away at an altitude of less than a dozen feet.

The first of the tracers passed in front of Hartley's plane, slamming into the old apartments to his left. The facade of the building collapsed in a heap of smoke and dust.

Hartley pivoted the plane right to face the oncoming Hind and pulled the trigger on his cannons. Nothing happened.

The Hind's next shots punched into the Harrier. Hartley's cockpit glass had two large holes the size of his fist punched into it. He aimed the nozzles towards the ground and pushed the throttle forward. The Harrier paused for a moment and then leapt upwards. The rest of the Hind's gunfire passed below his plane.

Hartley hoped for a miracle. Soon the Hind would be at point blank range. There would be no escaping its deadly cannons. The warning lights on his console flashed red and the engine whined. The alarms screamed in his earpiece.

He tried to get the altitude and speed up as well as he could. The Hind climbed to meet him, but Hartley's plane was faster. He flew over it and pickled his bomb switch again. Hartley closed his eyes knowing that one of three things would happen.

The first possibility was that the remaining cluster

bomb would explode on his hardpoint and destroy him. It was a unique form of suicide and one that he was sure would make the squadron commander grit his teeth while trying to write the letter back home to his parents, describing how their very stupid son had died.

The second possibility, and by far the most probable, was that he would pickle the remaining bomb and nothing would happen.

Neither occurred.

Hartley felt a bump as the Harrier ascended. The plane started to yaw a little in protest. Then he felt the weight of the cluster bomb suddenly drop off the plane. The aircraft soared upwards into the afternoon sky as if it had just been relieved of some terrible chronic malady.

The bomb canister fell off the Harrier's hardpoint and impacted with the rotors of the Hind. Spinning at 240 rpm, the blades of the rotor disintegrated as they encountered the bomb's hard metal casing. The 500-pound weapon was undeterred by the impact and continued its downwards journey into the fuselage of the Hind, which crumpled under its weight.

The Hind was carried downwards by the momentum of the bomb and plunged towards the street. By the time it reached the pavement ten meters below, the shell of the helicopter was split completely in two halves.

In one half, the pilot and gunner lay dead. In the other half, the fuel tank ruptured and spilled out its contents. Within seconds, the bomblets in the casing brewed up, exploding in a giant expanding ball of incandescent fury. The blast had enough force to level an entire city block.

The force of the explosion slapped into Hartley's plane. The Harrier's engine stopped completely. He kept the plane flying forwards with the throttle wide open, but the Harrier seemed to have just had enough.

The plane started to descend silently. There was not enough to altitude to eject. He steered the plane straight down the street, hoping for a controlled landing. He fought with the rudder and stick to keep the nose up. The pavement rushed up towards him.

As he landed, he heard the sickening crunch and the squeal of the plane's metal underbelly grinding along the asphalt. The Harrier skidded sideways to the right and Hartley felt the straps of his ejection seat dig into his shoulders.

The right wing slammed into a compact car and slid under the vehicle's body. It scooped up the little vehicle and pushed it along the street until it collided with the side of a truck. The Harrier stopped suddenly as it met the six-ton vehicle.

Hartley felt like he had just been worked over by Mike Tyson. He breathed hard and unbuckled. As he stood up in the cockpit, he realized he was sore but unhurt. In a daze, he half-climbed and half-fell from the Harrier.

The street far behind him was a river of fire. It was a sheer wall of flames for as far back as he could see. He grabbed his pistol and ran into a nearby supermarket. The electronic jingle of the doors happily welcomed him as he rushed in. He knew he was now in enemy territory and every second he was closer to being discovered.

Hartley hoped whoever came for him would be better prepared than he had been. He cocked the Browning, took a bite out of an apple that he nicked from the produce section.

Near the back of the store, he found an office. He was less than surprised when a lift of the receiver revealed that the line was dead. He sat in the old wooden desk chair, pondering of his next move.

10

Davis brought the Harrier down for a landing in the clearing of the woods just east of Rheda-Wiedenbrück. It was an emergency hide with no ops center or operations officer and only a handful of ground technicians. He shrugged his shoulders as he sat in the cockpit. *It will have to do.*

Nelson sat in the Harrier opposite him. He looked over at Davis silently. There was an accusation there somewhere, Davis was sure of it. He just wasn't sure of what. He had buried the hatchet with Hartley before the last mission.

In the air, there were no questions of his choices although of course Davis would have done things differently if he were in command. Now as the senior ranking officer, he was in charge of the flight. He would run things better, he was sure of it. *No more chances. Everyone gets back alive.*

Dunhill and Martin landed on the far side of the clearing and wheeled their Harriers in for a closer inspection by the ground crew. All the planes had signs of damage from the last mission but nothing quite so drastic as the earlier attack on the tank battalion east of Hannover. Davis credited himself for it.

Although he had gone too far with striking Hartley, he felt he had driven home his point about doing things by the book and preserving the Harriers and pilots of Shadow flight.

Nelson pulled a paperback out of his flight suit and resumed his reading. Davis watched the ground crew come in and check the aircraft. The radio was full of traffic but none of it with any news of Hartley. The trailers from the Bielefeld hide had turned southwest on the autobahn and were headed their way.

Davis shook his head, remembering how close the call had been trying to get away from the city. As they had just finished shutting down the Harrier engines, the first wave of helicopters buzzed over them. The bottom of the helicopter fuselages were only meters above where they sat in the cockpits.

The Rapier SAMs seemed to have been caught totally unaware and it was only when the second wave came in that it started to shoot at the helos from the top of the parking garage.

The first missiles found their targets, sending the Hinds to crash in a blazing heap on the streets far below. One of the Mi-24s slammed directly into the top floor of a nearby building and slid down the face of it.

Eventually, the Hinds noticed the Harrier hide for what it was and diverted several helicopters towards it. The helicopters came over slowly, firing volleys of rockets and spraying cannon fire at the top of the building. The two squads of guards fired back with handheld Blowpipe surface-to-air missiles.

True to the missile system's rumored performance, they all missed their targets. It was enough, however, to ward off the Hinds just long enough to keep them away from the top of the parking garage. The Harriers managed to tear away from the garage with their aircraft, if not their dignity, still intact.

Davis sat in his cockpit and waited for the next set of orders to roll in. This time, his flight would get it right.

The operations officer's runner arrived in his Land Rover. It was a young private named Harding. The Land Rover squealed to a stop and he ran out towards the Harrier. Davis beckoned him over.

"Close air support," Harding said in between breaths. "Hannover's fallen. Everyone on NORTHAG is pulling back towards the Weser."

Davis looked at the map and drew the new lines in with his grease pencil. The red line on the map showed the forward positions of NORTHAG. An area north of Kassel was circled with a red X.

"Belgians are falling back fast," Harding said. "They need some time and space to reorganize while they're pulling back."

Davis nodded. He watched the ground technicians jump out of the Unimog and rovers, newly arrived from their hasty evacuation from Bielefeld. They went to work, fitting the Harriers with SNEB rocket pods. Ten minutes later, Davis, Dunhill, Nelson, and Martin were in the air.

"Alright, gents. We have no room for mistakes here," declared Davis. "Follow my lead, keep low, and hit the target out from as far away as you can. No heroics. No second passes. If something doesn't look right, we leave immediately."

Nelson was quiet, as usual. Dunhill seemed eager. "Roger that, we'll give those bastards something to think about," he said.

Martin radioed back an affirmative. Davis could swear he heard the tremor in the lad's voice, but he knew it was impossible to hear things that clearly over their patchy radio connection. They flew to the southeast, keeping low.

"Sunshine Flight to Eyes, can you read me?" Davis spoke to the AWACS plane circling to the west. "Any hostiles inbound to our position?"

"Be advised we have heavy air traffic in your area," came the response. "Offensive counter-air operations are underway. I have two BARCAP flights near you. They are on call and available for intercept if needed." The AWACS controller gave them a vector and a radio frequency for the friendly fighter aircraft.

Davis thought to himself how much more organized and calm the AWACS response sounded. Having a combat air patrol on call was something new too. It sounded like NATO was slowly overcoming the initial shock of the Warsaw Pact invasion early this morning.

The terrain in the Belgian I Corps sector was much hillier and more forested than the plains near Hannover. Davis was struck by how much more energy it took to keep the plane flying at low level.

Once the Harriers arrived on station, Davis found the frequency for the forward air controller and announced their presence.

"Sunshine, we are requesting support near Wilhelmshöhe. Coordinates follow," the Belgian controller said.

Davis checked his map and found the coordinates on his navigation system.

"Sunshine to Kestrel, I have that location as Bergpark, is that correct?" asked Davis.

The response came quickly. "Affirmative, that's the national park. There is a tank regiment on the southeast of the park engaged with friendly units on the north side of the park. Request assistance immediately. Yellow smoke marks the friendly lines."

The Harrier flight sped east towards the park. The tall spire of the Hercules monument came into view. Black smoke rose up from where the building stood. Davis' radar warning lit up. His Harrier followed the long slope that descended east towards the city of Kassel. A puff of smoke to his right announced the presence of the enemy's fire. Davis pulled left as the alarm blared in his ear.

"SAM launch! I have a SAM launch!" He twisted the plane left in a sharp turn and dropped flares and chaff behind him.

"Come left, Sunshine! Left!" he heard Nelson yell.

Davis shoved the flight stick and the Harrier started a roll. For a moment, it seemed like it might not be recoverable. He brought the stick back right, but the Harrier kept rolling. Davis watched the ground come up fast towards him.

He pressed hard on the rudder and gulped air as the Harrier's roll slowly halted and reversed. When the aircraft finally righted, his plane was less than a dozen feet off the ground.

Dunhill chimed in. "By god, if you'd been flying on flat ground, you'd be dead, Sunshine!"

Davis felt the shake of the aircraft as he sped over the park. The SAM had missed him, but he felt the sweat pour down his face and neck. It spilled down his back and he whispered to himself, trying to regain his nerve. *Yellow smoke. Find the yellow smoke.*

"I can't see it," he said to the flight. "Anyone see the smoke?"

Silence.

"I'm getting pasted by flak," announced Martin. "Still okay to fly though."

The flight was soon past the park and over Kassel. Davis turned back north for home. *One pass. That's it. We looked for your smoke and it wasn't there.*

"Sunshine to Kestrel, we didn't see your smoke," said Davis.

The forward air controller came back on the radio twenty seconds later. "Sorry, Sunshine, a delay there. We have the smoke out now."

Davis shook his head. "Sunshine Flight, let's return to base."

Nelson's voice shouted him down. "You can't be serious! Those men down there need us!" he said. "Turn around! Come on!"

Davis watched the hills ahead of him. The words shot out of him. "You heard me," he said. "Return to base."

Nelson came back on the radio. "Negative, Sunshine. I'm leaving formation. Wish me luck. Over."

The red-hot rage welled up within Davis. "Get back here, Horatio! That is a direct order!"

No response. Davis looked back to where Nelson should have been and found only empty air in his place.

"Hell!" Davis swung the aircraft around, driven by hot anger. Underneath all the rules and regulations that he had striven so hard to uphold since the accident, a part of him understood that it was all just a means of coping, of staying afloat despite being blameless in a tragedy that happened so long ago.

As he saw the sparks of triple-A light up over the park, he wondered if it was ever too late for a man to change.

11

Spencer wolfed down the chicken sandwich. He hated field rations, but he was hungry and it was the first real meal he had had all day.

"How did it happen?" he asked Jones, pointing to where Stewart's corpse lay.

Jones scooped up some spaghetti sauce from his rations and hesitated. "We had him in our sights from two hundred meters. The bastards were onto him nearly from the moment he landed. Your friend was badly injured from the crash but conscious. When they caught up to him, he played dead and shot the first one who found him."

Spencer felt a little warmer knowing that Stewart managed to put up a fight on the way down. It was the way he would have wanted it.

"So the second one got him right away?" asked Spencer.

"Negative," said Jones. "Willis took a shot from where

he was hiding and drilled the next one in the forehead. After that, they all came running."

Spencer nodded, realizing that the shots from Stewart and Willis had surely saved his skin while he was hiding in the bush, injured and terrified. He thought of all the times that Stewart had been the butt of his jokes.

How often had he thoroughly enjoyed needlessly antagonizing the man in the name of fun? And after all that, the big angry Scot had ended up saving his life. Spencer felt the lump rising in his throat and pushed it down deep inside of him.

Jones continued. "There were just too many of them. Stewart fired back and clipped one of the buggers who got too close. The rest of them unloaded on him. He took two more out before they got him. It was a grenade that finally ended it."

"How did you manage to get Stewart's body out?" Spencer asked.

Jones pointed toward Willis, who sat in the rover dozing. "Once the Puma came in, almost everyone ran off to the other side of the road. Willis hit the remaining ones and the rest of us pulled Stewart out of the cockpit. No one gets left behind, right?"

Spencer thought about the expertise and timing that the whole operation must have required. These men were clearly not regular army. The question leapt into his head. "Are you fellows from the SAS?" he asked.

Jones looked around at the three other men. "Not quite but you're close enough," he said.

Spencer nodded. The tone in Jones' voice gave off the distinct feeling that this line of inquiry would go no further.

"When can I...we...go home?" Spencer asked. He looked over towards where Stewart lay.

Jones set the can down and walked over to the Land Rover. One of the other men sat in the truck talking on the radio. A minute later, Jones returned to where Spencer sat. "We've got a Puma heading this way for a pickup in about ten minutes. We'll take you to the right spot soon enough."

The talk of the Puma made Spencer think of the helicopter that came to rescue him earlier. The pilots were smarter than he had given them credit for. "Drawing Ivan off to the other side of the road like that was a bloody good idea," he said. "My compliments to the pilot."

Jones chuckled. "You can tell them that yourself when they come get you," he said. "We're leaving in three minutes." The short broad soldier tossed him a tattered facecloth. "You may want to clean your face up a bit, sir. You look like hell."

Spencer walked over to the Land Rover and sat in the front seat. He pulled out a small dirty mirror from his rescue kit. The shock set in immediately when he saw his own face. *Blood. I'm covered in another man's blood.*

His mind flashed to the man he had killed with his knife in the forest clearing. Turning his head to the side, he leaned from the vehicle and threw up the contents of his lunch on the ground. The breaths came out in short sharp heaves.

A few seconds later, a canteen was thrust towards him. His hands trembled as the water gushed out, soaking the cotton material. Spencer closed his eyes and wiped his face and neck. He scrubbed again and again and his body trembled and shivered as he wiped the blood off. *Clean. Clean. I've got to get clean.*

Spencer was still wiping his face as the Land Rover's engine started and the vehicle pulled out of the clearing. He was not a religious man but he wondered a little if he would be judged for what he had done. Knowing that it was either him or the enemy, he felt a little assured.

But what about all those enemy soldiers who he had killed with the cluster bombs? They had roasted to death in the back of those armored vehicles. How was he so affected by killing one man with a knife and not the hundreds of men with a bomb? *No. They put the uniform on this morning - just like me.*

But other questions replaced that one. Why had Stewart died and not him? Among the two, Stewart was undoubtedly the better man. He had a family - a wife and a son back home. Spencer had no one. He had spent his entire life keeping people at a distance. If anyone should have been killed back there, he was surely karma's prime candidate.

Now the war didn't seem like quite the adventure anymore. No one got what they deserved. The war stories he had read as a child...it wasn't that they were untrue - but they certainly didn't tell the whole story, did they?

Something shifted inside of Spencer and he wasn't sure how to deal with it. As the Land Rover traversed over the bumpy fields, he was jolted back to reality. At last Spencer brokered a truce within himself. *I am alive. It is good to be alive.*

Five minutes later, they arrived at a countryside farm that had long been abandoned. Wrecked T-72s and Chieftain tanks lay smouldering in the fields. Deep pits had been hammered into the ground by an artillery barrage.

Bodies were scattered among the debris, twisted and unrecognizable. The smell of burning fuel filled Spencer's nostrils. The four soldiers with him stopped the Land Rover in the middle of the field and waited.

Spencer was unnerved by the sights of the battle and the deathly quiet around him. He calmed down by telling himself that whatever had happened here had clearly moved on. The Soviets were far to the west now and the next echelon was still marshalling to the east. They were in a little peaceful pocket behind enemy lines.

The Puma came in low and descended towards a small dirt road about 100 meters away. Spencer got out and Jones walked him over to the descending helo. The rotor wash was strong and pushed him a little as he limped the distance to the Puma.

The door slid open and the crew chief beckoned them inside. Spencer felt a wave of both relief and tremendous guilt spill over him as he entered the rear compartment of the helicopter.

He sat down on the floor and looked outside towards Jones as he walked away. He hoped the man would look back one more time, but he kept walking and climbed in the Land Rover. The vehicle pulled away as the helicopter slowly ascended.

Twenty-five minutes later, Spencer had crossed back

over friendly lines and landed at a field hospital near Munster.

For now, his war was over.

12

Nelson scanned the horizon to the south as the radar warning receiver chirped in his ear. The Harrier was slow to respond to his commands with the added weight of the SNEB rockets under his wing. He ignored the steady stream of curses and threats from Davis that flooded over his radio.

Somewhere down there, the Belgians were dying and he was the only one who could help. He knew it sounded arrogant, but this happened to be war and he knew it would be acts like this that decided its outcome.

If he were shot down, another man would take his place. And another. There would always be men like Davis too. And maybe that was alright. But that didn't mean he had to follow just anyone. In the end, he was also partly responsible for what happened down there on the ground. He would accept the consequences of dropping out of formation and completing the mission as ordered.

Nelson looked for the yellow smoke that marked the appearance of friendly lines. He brought the Harrier west to avoid Kassel where the Soviets were already firmly in control and bringing their anti-air assets into play.

A line of anti-aircraft artillery shot up beside him. He banked right and kept scanning for the smoke. The Harrier jumped suddenly and he heard a thud against the fuselage. His radar started beeping loudly at him and he brought the Harrier down to the double digits of altitude, skimming dangerously low to the slope of the park as he ascended.

At the top of the long hill he saw the Hercules Monument come up fast towards him and he climbed at a nearly 90-degree angle of attack to avoid the large castle-like structure. In the rear-view mirror, he spotted the explosion as the SAM that was chasing him hit the spire.

He circled back. *Third time's lucky.* His Harrier came in low again, this time descending the slope. He gritted his teeth and hoped for the best. Suddenly, it came into view. There was a little puff of a yellow cloud along the treeline to the south. Nelson smiled. *There. There it is.*

He rolled the Harrier over to the left and fired. The rockets rippled out from their pods laying down a long carpet of explosions. Smoke and dust filled the air.

His radio crackled. "Sunshine to Horatio, we are on station. Do you have a visual on the smoke?"

Nelson opened his mouth to reply but something very hard slapped against his Harrier. He reached for the ejection handle, but the fireball swept over him before he could do anything.

13

The abandoned civilian vehicles along the street were consumed by the detonation of the cluster bomb's 147 bomblets and the unlucky Hind helicopter that had been underneath the Harrier as the time of their release.

Hartley took another bite of the delicious apple and mulled over his options. He could stay here and be captured or killed by the airmobile troops that were operating in the city - or he could find a vehicle and get the hell out of here as fast as possible.

He checked his kneeboard map and figured out the distance and route to the nearest friendlies. By now, the West Germans would be fully aware of what had happened here. His best bet was that the Bundeswehr would be sending troops east along Route 2.

He could meet them along the way, get debriefed, and return to the flight by evening. Now all he needed was a car, of which there were plenty available outside. Unfortunately, they were all of the "on fire" variety.

Hartley walked out of the supermarket and rushed along Potsdamer Strasse. The neatly trimmed lawns and well-kept houses of the city on either side of the street stood desolate and empty. In the distance, he heard the rattle of gunfire. Apparently, the city was not entirely defenseless.

It was leaning against the white two-storey home. Hartley smiled and sprinted across the road towards the Maico motorcycle. He had a 490 back home before his ex-wife had forced him to sell it. This one was a pretty little green and red 400. It was an older model from 1979 but it was still impressive. The keys were in the ignition. Hartley couldn't believe his luck.

He grabbed the bike and slammed his foot down on the kickstart. The little engine sputtered and died. He tried again. Nothing. On the third try, the bike's engine didn't so much as cough. Hartley was crestfallen.

He let the bike drop to the ground. A rapid stream of very quiet but very angry German words flowed out from behind him. As he turned, the hard metal pressed into the back of his neck. Hartley stuck his hands up slowly.

"Don't move, you bastard," he heard in German. It was a male's voice, deep and thick with the threat of immediate violence.

Hartley spoke up. "RAF. Squadron Leader John Hartley," he said. "Englander."

The pressure on his neck did not slacken. A hand reached around him and pulled his Browning from the holster he wore. Another German voice came from further behind him. He was turned around to face a pair of middle-aged man wearing olive drab uniforms and berets with a leaf cluster. The man closest to him had a stern expression on his face and he stepped back with his nine millimeter raised and ready.

Hartley recognized the men immediately for what they were.

Territorialheer. Thank god.

Hartley tried to speak a little German. He cursed himself for not taking the language courses more seriously. In peacetime, he could manage a brief introduction, talk about his hobbies, and even maybe pick up a German girl in town if she found his attempts at speaking the local language funny and endearing.

But here with a pistol raised to his head, he couldn't manage more than a flailing attempt at speaking. The only word that came to him was "Jagdflieger" - fighter pilot. He pointed to himself and said the word repeatedly, feeling like a total idiot at the same time.

The German men conferred with one another. Finally, the furthest of the two shouted towards him. "Maybe it's better to speak in English," he said.

"Look, I'm a pilot. I was shot down over the city," Hartley said. "I need to get out of here. Can you help me?"

The closer of the two German men said nothing but his expression slackened just enough to put Hartley at ease. Suddenly, he remembered his German, but it was useless now. The moment had passed.

There was a flood of quick German spoken between the two men. Hartley couldn't catch much of it. The closer of the two took a step back and pointed the pistol away from Hartley. The Browning was not returned.

"I'm Werner," the man who had been holding the pistol to Hartley's head said. He pointed to the man who stood behind him. "This is Schmidt."

Hartley thought about shaking their hands and then thought better of it. "Maybe we should get out of the road here and go somewhere else?" he suggested.

Schmidt nodded and the three of them walked into the nearby house. Inside were the signs of panicked packing. Clothes and toys were strewn about over the kitchen. Cupboard doors were left open and various food items left out. Towels were piled high on the kitchen table.

The three men sat down. Schmidt wiped his arm across the table, sweeping all the various items off the table top and onto the floor. They clattered on the linoleum. Hartley tried hard not to look at the photos of the family that were framed and hung in the kitchen and on the wall of the nearby hallway. He resisted the urge to wonder where they were now or if they were even alive.

Werner pulled out a map from his pack and unfolded it on the table. Using a grease pencil, he marked their current location. "You're best to avoid the autobahn," he said. "From what I've heard it's too crowded right now."

Hartley shook his head. "That's just what I was planning to do, actually. What do you recommend besides that?"

"That's easy," said Schmidt. "Northwest on Route 68 and then 33 to Osnabruck. That's where I'll bet the counterattack is coming from. You'd better leave now if you're to avoid the worst of it."

The sounds of automatic rifle fire and explosions outside were several blocks away by Hartley's estimate. It had grown louder and more intense since he had left the supermarket. Time seemed short and something didn't seem right about these two men.

"What were you two doing?" Hartley asked. "Just strolling by the neighborhood? Isn't most of the fighting to the south of here? Near the city center?"

Schmidt bristled at what the question implied. "We are reservists," he said. "This morning when the fighting started, we waited and waited for the order to mobilize. Nothing came. So we have been going door-to-door and mobilizing the ones who are still here."

Hartley tried to suppress the question in his mind, but he couldn't resist asking. "What's the meaning of the Soviets tasking an airmobile operation for Bielefeld? What do they want from here that's worth it all?"

Schmidt and Werner looked at each other seriously. "Two reasons. One is likely to cut off the supplies going towards the front." Hartley nodded. It made sense, especially since Route 2 going east from here was clearly one of the fastest ways to get the supply trucks through.

With that route cut off, the NATO defenders would need to rely on the local roads, which were only one or two lanes in places, not to mention crowded with refugee traffic flowing west. If supplies were the lifeblood of an army, the autobahn was like the major arteries it moved along. You might manage to survive without them, but not for very long.

"What's the other reason?" asked Hartley.

"POMCUS," said Werner. Hartley knew what he was referring to. POMCUS was the NATO acronym that referred to pre-positioned equipment that was placed throughout West Germany and the Low Countries.

In case of war in Europe, American personnel would be flown over here and find their tanks and vehicles already waiting for them. The general location of the POMCUS sites was already known and security was very tight. Hartley couldn't remember hearing about a POMCUS site near Bielefeld though.

"A POMCUS site? This far forward? You've got to be kidding me! The Americans are far south of here anyways. It makes no sense!" said Hartley.

Werner shrugged. "You didn't consider that other countries - such as your own - would also have POMCUS sites here too? Bremerhaven will soon be overrun. Don't you think your government would have considered that happening? They had forty years."

Of course. Surely if the Americans had made plans for their equipment to be pre-positioned in the case of war, it made sense for the British to do the same.

Although gaining access to the continent seemed like a simple manner of crossing the channel, there were no guarantees that the Soviets wouldn't have their submarines infesting the waters around the UK, just hoping that the British government was foolish enough to ship its equipment over after the war had already begun.

Bielefeld was dangerously close to British I Corps's front line though. It seemed like a huge gamble to put equipment so close to the Inner German border. A part of

Hartley admired the guts it took to do it.

"Look, I had no idea about this POMCUS site until you told me just now," said Hartley. "I've got clearance too. So pray tell how the Russians knew about it."

Schmidt shook his head. "No one really knows. The prisoners we've taken so far haven't survived long enough to tell us that."

Hartley tried to keep the implications of the statement out of his mind. "What have they told you? Did they find the site?"

Schmidt shook his head. "Even we don't know where it is exactly. It's likely underground somewhere but where exactly? Who knows? Probably not even the Russians. What's important is that they know there's something here and they're keeping you from using it against them."

The sound of the fighting was getting closer.

Hartley stood up and poured some water from the tap into a glass and drank. It would have been a good time for tea, especially after hearing such news. Not only was Bielefeld a convenient place for Harriers to hide, it was also a nice place to stow tons of weapons and vehicles that may be the key to salvaging the northern front in Germany. Hartley wasn't sure when the reinforcements were scheduled to arrive, but it was likely in the next 24 hours or so.

Could the fate of the war really rest on such secrets? It seemed desperate.

But such a word perfectly described the situation the world was in right now. And if the Russians did manage to find the POMCUS site then what? Would they destroy it or would they try to use the equipment for themselves?

Hartley tried to picture the chaos that would be created by hundreds of British tanks full of Russian soldiers prowling around NATO's rear. It wouldn't take much to create a total collapse of morale - not to mention the havoc it would create with command and control.

"I need to get out of here right away," Hartley said. "Did you radio anyone? Did you mention that the Russians were here looking for the POMCUS site?"

Werner shook his head. "Jamming and lots of it," he said. "They must have brought along some kind of radio interference device with them. Ever since they landed, we've been unable to contact anyone at 3rd Panzer Division. Phone lines are down all around the city too."

That settled it for Hartley. He stuck out his hand towards Schmidt. "My Browning, please?"

Schmidt handed it back to him. "Are you sure you don't want anything a little heavier?" he asked. "Plenty of bad guys out there."

Hartley shook his head. "I'm not a good shot even with my pistol. I'd hate to think about what I couldn't hit with a rifle or submachine gun."

They walked outside the house and Hartley pointed to the Maico. "If you can get me up and running on this thing, I should be able to make it out of the city without even firing a shot. What do you say?"

Both Germans looked over the motorcycle and checked the engine over. Schmidt disappeared into the garage and walked back with a handful of wrenches. After a few twists and turns on the engine mounting, he found enough space to get his fingers in and adjust the timing chain.

Hartley tried to start the bike. The engine sputtered in protest the first time, but the second good kick got it running. The motorcycle didn't quite purr as much as it hammered. It was not beautiful by any means but the bike's 247cc engine and off-road tires were what he really required. He sat on the motorcycle, feeling the bike vibrate beneath him.

Schmidt and Werner waved and Hartley drove the bike off down the street towards Route 68. On the way there, he wondered if he would see either men again. Somehow, he doubted it. War was just like that.

The sounds of fighting disappeared behind him. He passed by the city center and ducked as he turned one corner only to find a group of Soviet airmobile soldiers in the street.

One of them fired at him. The tracers cut into the convenience store behind him. Hartley gunned the engine and turned around as fast as the bike could carry him. He turned left at the intersection, under fire the whole way.

A few blocks west, he found the turn to Route 68. The entrance to the highway was clogged with abandoned civilian vehicles. Hartley reckoned the occupants had been caught in the miles-long traffic jam going out of the city and simply decided to take their chances on foot or back in Bielefeld. Either option would have been safer than being out on the open road during a battle.

He angled the bike around the cars, threading the

needle between bumpers at times while driving along the crumbling narrow strip of pavement on the right edge of the road at others. Osnabruck was 50 kilometers away - a half hour's pleasant drive on a nice day but an arduous journey in the middle of a war.

In frustration, he brought the bike down into the fields and drove it along the dirt paths and bumpy uncultivated farmland west of Bielefeld. The going wasn't much faster than the highway, but it was certainly less frustrating. Hartley imagined himself as that most American of actors - Steve McQueen in The Great Escape.

Only this time, the soldiers and the death and the desperation were all extremely real.

14

Davis shook as he watched Nelson's plane turn into a ball of flame. The smoke trail of the SAM lingered in the sky and the fragments of the aircraft fell to earth. The lump in his throat grew as he brought the Harrier down lower and lower until he could see the distinct features of the ground clearly ahead of him.

The forward air controller reported good hits on Nelson's last run. Davis could see the yellow smoke below him, showing the position of friendly troops. There was a pall of smoke and dust wafting over the park where the Nelson's SNEB rockets had hit.

Much of the foliage was burning and clumps of vehicles could be seen rolling away from the conflagration. It was these vehicles that Davis decided to shoot his rockets at, hoping to catch whoever had fired the missile that took Nelson's life.

Dunhill and Martin were behind him, following his lead. The rockets spat out from their pods. As they impacted the ground and vehicles below, the air filled with smoke and debris. Visibility was nil. They were reduced to hoping that their jets wouldn't impact head-on with any unexpected obstacles. A second later, they emerged from the cloud.

The forward air controller's voice poured over the radio. "This is Kestrel. Nice shooting today. Thanks for the assistance."

Davis could hardly speak as he brought the Harrier northwest, heading for home. Dunhill and Martin kept their usual banter to a minimum. They would all need to deal with the losses today. Thinking about it seemed overwhelming enough.

As he flew low over friendly airspace, Davis thought about Nelson's reckless decision to disobey orders and turn back. By returning to the target area alone after overflying it once, he had sealed his fate. The SAM and AAA operators were ready for him and Nelson paid for the decision with his life. Davis couldn't shake the nagging feeling that the young pilot had made the right decision.

The flight landed in the field near a nice flat stretch of road that could be used for short take-offs. The Harriers drove along the steel planks and parked among the tall trees. Davis clambered from his cockpit and found his legs after a quick stretch.

Dunhill strode up to Davis with his hands on his hips. "Bloody fool that Nelson," he said quietly. "The target wasn't marked. We had every right to turn off home."

Davis nodded and watched him walk off. Martin sat in his cockpit eating a chocolate bar. The technicians went to work examining the aircraft and pulling the empty rocket pods off the Harrier's hardpoints.

"How'd you find it out there?" Davis shouted up to Martin.

Martin leaned down from the cockpit and bit off the last chunk of chocolate. He let the wind take the plastic wrapper.

"As good as it gets," Martin replied. "Only wish I could have gone back for a third run and watched the secondaries. Must have looked incredible on the ground." He laughed to himself and leaned back in his seat.

Davis walked off towards the makeshift latrine. How could men who were trained in the same manner and tactics have such a vastly different reaction to danger? He tried to stow the questions away as he relieved himself in solitude.

Five minutes later, he went into the big boxy Marshall Cabin and gave a debriefing over the telecommunications system to Briscoe. The operations officer sounded exhausted and overwhelmed. Davis wasn't sure what to say about Nelson, so he merely stated the facts of what had happened.

If there was any official disapproval or vindication over Davis's decisions, he couldn't tell from Briscoe's response. It brought no relief. It only meant that Davis would have to make sense of it all on his own.

"How are things going elsewhere?" Davis asked.

"We're pulling back west over the Weser before nightfall," said Briscoe. "There's been some trouble in Bielefeld that we're hoping to clear up, as you know. We've had to reroute supplies towards Hannover because of it."

Davis felt the sting of Hartley's loss. A big part of him hoped that he would return here safely, if only to resume the leadership of the flight. Davis wasn't sure he wanted it anymore after the previous mission.

"Belgians are pulling back from Kassel now," said Briscoe. "Looks like you and a few other CAS flights managed to buy enough time for the West Germans to get in position behind them. Well done."

Davis asked no more questions. Briscoe signed off, warning them to get ready for another flight soon. A West German counterattack was being prepared to retake Bielefeld. "Your Harriers will be supporting it," he said.

With that, Davis left the cabin and walked back to his Harrier. His body was stiff from sitting in the Harrier cockpit all day. How many sorties had he flown now today? And it was not even three in the afternoon yet.

It had been a hell of a war so far.

15

Hartley found the highway leading northwest to Osnabruck much more easy going. The Maico had been faithful to him so far, carrying him over the uneven fields and pastures. He was glad to leave them behind though as the bike's tires found an easy grip on the pavement of Route 33.

The supply convoys full of NATO trucks passed by him on the other side of the roadway. Abandoned civilian vehicles had merely been shoved aside by heavy construction vehicles.

Hartley knew that these convoys would need to be routed much further south along the smaller and more clogged road network to reach the defenders south of Hannover. Even if the Russians were unable to find the POMCUS site, taking Bielefeld had been a sound operational move.

As he got closer to the city, he began to wonder what kind of force would be assembled to retake the city. The UK 12th Armored Brigade was headquartered there but had probably been deployed east of the Weser since this morning.

Whoever was coming for Bielefeld would need plenty of tanks and men. The Russians seemed to have an entire regiment there already, judging by the number of Hinds he had seen earlier.

Reaching the outskirts of the city, he swung the bike towards Hannoversche Street. The tall stony towers of St. Peter's Cathedral plunged upwards over the city's skyline. As he rode down the wide avenue towards the inner city, he saw a group of Leopard tanks rolling towards him. A traffic warden and several police officers beckoned at pedestrians to stop. Hartley drove straight towards the Leopard tanks despite the police whistles.

Hartley let the Maico clatter to the street and waved his arms wildly at the lead tank. The commander stopped the tank while ordering the others in the group to halt. Behind them were more Leopards quickly approaching. Clearly this was not the time nor place for a conversation.

The tank commander wore the beret of the Territorialheer. He waved at Hartley to come up to talk to him. Hartley stepped up onto the tank chassis and the Leopard's engine sputtered loudly as it went back into gear and continued its rolling down the street.

Hartley gripped a steel handle on the turret. The tank commander, who wore the rank of captain on his epaulets, looked at him expectantly. Hartley felt relieved, knowing the man was probably the leader of the whole squadron.

"RAF. My name's Hartley," he introduced himself. "I was shot down over Bielefeld. Is that where you're going now?"

The captain nodded. Hartley was relieved that he understood his English even over the clatter of the tank engine. "The Russians are looking for something very important there," said Hartley. "They may be trying to find a load of British equipment - vehicles, tanks, weapons."

The commander looked at him, surprise written across his face. Hartley nodded. "You need to tell someone about that right now because if they find those tanks, it's bad news."

The commander reached down into the turret and started speaking in German on the radio. He spoke for a few minutes and Hartley sat on the turret. When the tank commander was finally done speaking on the radio, he asked a few questions about the disposition of Russian troops in the city. Hartley confessed he didn't know much but he had only seen infantry and helicopters. "Lots of helicopters and men," he said.

"If it's not too much trouble, I'd like to get back to my squadron," said Hartley. "I'm sure they're wondering where I am."

The tank commander nodded and told Hartley to get off. "Someone will be here soon to help you with that," he said. Hartley jumped off the tank and watched the long line of armor pass by. A few minutes later, a three-ton truck rolled up towards where he stood. One of the officers, a colonel of the 12th Armored Division jumped out from the passenger seat to meet him.

"I understand you're one of the Harrier pilots from number four squadron," the colonel said, shaking Hartley's hand. "I've spoken with Wing Commander Madison already. We have a helo waiting to take you to your hide.

Get in, please."

The colonel's aide threw the Land Rover into gear and turned left towards a flat grassy park.

Hartley felt the relief wash over him. Soon he would be back with his flight. "Looks like you'll have your hands full, sir," he said. "The Russians - they're after the POMCUS site in Bielefeld."

A look of shock and alarm spread over the colonel's tired face. "If they destroy it, that's bad enough," said the colonel. "But if they decide to use the equipment…"

"Well, when I left, they hadn't found it yet but sure as hell they know it's there," said Hartley. "The local Heer told me they captured one of the bastards and he admitted they were looking for it, sir. Even the Germans didn't know where it was."

The colonel nodded thoughtfully. "That information was kept very secret," he said. "Seems like it wasn't kept secret enough."

"Sir, I know the location of the site is beyond my clearance," said Hartley. "But can you tell me what kind of equipment and how much is sitting at the site?"

The colonel coughed, visibly uncomfortable to even be asked such a question. "It's a regiment's worth. They were earmarked for a category II reserve armor regiment. That's already more than I should say."

Hartley did the math by himself. "Maybe more than 100 vehicles then," he said. "Colonel, can you at least tell me what I'm looking for? Vehicle types, maybe?"

The colonel remained silent as the land rover made its way through the park. The driver was quite adept at his job and swerved the vehicle around trees while he drove over the grass. At other times, he kept the vehicle on the narrow pedestrian walkways that were empty of civilians.

The West German Bell Huey helicopter sat on a clear stretch of grass with its rotors spinning. Hartley got out of the Rover, trying to shake off the frustration. He took a step towards the helicopter and felt a hand on his shoulder. The colonel tugged at Hartley's sleeve.

"It's a light armored regiment," the old man said. "You're looking for Strikers and Scorpions mainly. Not much armor but they pack a solid punch with anti-tank missiles."

Hartley nodded. "I just hope the Germans don't get too bogged down with retaking the city if the Russians find the POMCUS site in time."

He hopped on the Huey and it took off south towards Munster. Flying low over the mostly flat terrain, he was elated to be back in the air again - even if he wasn't the one piloting the aircraft.

The Huey set down near the Harrier hide. For the three remaining Harrier pilots of Shadow Flight, his return was akin to the second coming. Davis looked positively ecstatic upon Hartley's arrival.

"Good to have you back here, Hartley," he said. "Some bad news about Nelson though. Shot down near Kassel."

Hartley felt a wave of nausea pass over him. "See any chute?" he asked with a hopeful tone in his voice.

Dunhill looked away as Davis shook his head. "No. No chance at all," he said.

Hartley steadied himself as the ground fell out between his feet. He rested his hand on a nearby table and sat down. "Bloody hell, what a day. Stewart, Spencer, Bellamy, Nelson…how many else are we going to lose?"

The operations officer's runner sprinted up to them. "Your planes are ready," he said. "You'd better get going."

16

Hartley knew from the look on Dunhill's face that things weren't good. He suspected it had something to do with the last mission under Davis's command. And it more than likely had something to do with the way Nelson had bought it.

He wasn't sure what to do about it now. There was simply not time to address it. *In the end, we're all professionals. We can keep things together long enough to pull through this next mission.*

Flying north towards Bielefeld, he checked his navigation system and noted the range and distance to the city. It was coming up in only a matter of minutes. The West Germans were already on the way and would be there any minute.

Hartley wasn't a big fan of dropping ordnance in a city on a close air support mission. It was the most dangerous mission to pull off and had a high likelihood of killing the wrong people.

"Anyone joining us on this outing?" asked Martin.

Hartley watched the ground slide quickly by his plane. "Word from ops is that most of our planes are doing heavy counter-air right now. Pact airfields are getting hit hard."

"Well, that's fine and dandy but who's covering the troops right now?" he asked.

Hartley chuckled. "Mostly close air support and interdiction around Hannover and near Kassel," he said. "That pretty much leaves us and a few Lynx helicopters. The West Germans have a bit of artillery. Otherwise, it's just us right now."

"I don't like it," said Davis. "Sounds like a recipe for disaster."

Dunhill chimed in. "Disaster? Hardly. I would use that word to describe the spot of trouble we ran into on the last run."

There was a tense silence over the radio. Hartley worried that things would collapse if he continued to say nothing. "Gentlemen," he said firmly. "Steady on. Let's get this thing done, shall we? We'll sort things out among us later."

The rest of the flight north was quiet. Hartley changed the frequency on the net over to listen to the West German reserve unit closing in on the city. Hartley brought the flight around east of Bielefeld first and circled counter clockwise to the north. The Soviet helicopters were long gone but the city bore the scars of battle now.

Several of the taller buildings in the small city had

collapsed and there were entire blocks in the suburbs that appeared levelled. A square blanket of ash replaced the peaceful neighborhoods.

Fires had broken out and appeared scattered across the city. The smoke poured up from everywhere, it seemed, and Hartley wondered how the hell they would ever provide accurate support from up here.

The radar warning receiver was thankfully silent. It may have been due to a complete lack of surface-to-air weapons but more likely it was due to the low altitude flying around the city. Hartley had a hunch that the missiles would pop off if they flew over Bielefeld.

The Territorialheer were busy chatting on the radio in German. Hartley caught a few disconnected words here and there but couldn't really make sense of it.

"Anyone catch that?" he asked the flight.

Dunhill piped up. "They're approaching the outskirts of the city from the west," he said. "Sounds like they're attempting to link up with German reservists already there. Appears the Leopards are meeting light resistance."

"I can see artillery hitting down there," said Martin. "Looks like someone's taking a right pasting."

Hartley watched the balls of black smoke being thrown up from the ground off his left wing. "Let's stay in formation circling now," he said. "Don't go off trying to hit targets of opportunity. Especially when we haven't ID'ed what's down there."

"They're entering the city," Dunhill announced. Lots of excited German voices could be heard over the frequency.

"Those Leopards are getting hit by RPGs at close range."

Hartley resisted the urge to bring the flight in for a closer look. He had learned something from the earlier missions. If something didn't feel right, it was better to hold back and wait for things to develop.

Dunhill spoke up. "Sounds like they're taking a beating," he said.

"Let's get in there! What are we waiting for?!" shouted Martin.

Hartley ignored him. "If they ask for it, we'll be there. In the meantime, let's keep well away from it. Circling around there will only tip our hand. When we go in, we'll come from the east, where we can surprise the hell out of them."

The four Harriers hugged the ground to the north. Hartley swung the plane around and headed back southeast. He circled low over the autobahn on the east side of the small city. The chatter from the West Germans in the city grew louder and more intense. Hartley checked the radar warning receiver and got nothing.

A quick chat with the AWACs controller revealed skies clear of enemy planes within a forty-kilometer radius of his position. Hartley smiled at the thought of NATO's offensive counter air missions hitting the Russians.

"Shadow this is Tupper, are you seeing what I'm seeing? On the ground at your three," said Martin.

Hartley glanced toward the ground. Everything was going by in the usual blur. He pulled back on the throttle and turned the Harrier into a tight circle. Looking down, he watched a blob of tan vehicles move slowly along the autobahn towards the west.

"Jesus, is that what I think that is?" asked Dunhill.

"Looks like a formation of vehicles," said Davis. "West German?"

Hartley brought the plane in low and swept over the vehicles at a height of less than a dozen feet. The tracers jumped up towards him. He looked in his rear-view mirror. The color and shape were all familiar to him. His heart sank.

"Looks like those Ivan's have found the POMCUS site," said Hartley. "Sod it."

Hartley rolled his eyes at the situation. The West German armor was caught up in the city with the Russians inside delaying its advance for as long as it could. Instead of fighting to hold onto the city, they had merely been buying time for the men in the POMCUS raid to get away from Bielefeld and head east.

Very soon, an entire regiment's worth of British vehicles manned by enemy soldiers would slam head on into the NATO defender's rear. Chaos and destruction would inevitably ensue.

He squirmed in his cockpit at the thought and brought the flight low to the north.

"Well gents, it appears to be just us right now," Hartley told the men in the flight. "If these blokes find the NATO rear, they won't last long but I imagine they won't mind too much. They'll have carved an opportunity for their mates on the other side of the lines to punch through."

"What do you propose?" asked Davis. "Think these SNEBS will manage to do the job?"

Hartley keyed his radio. "I'm sure they will," he said. "Light armored vehicles. We should be able to take them. The trick is getting them in a bunch. They'd be foolish to stay on the autobahn. Look - they're already fanning out over the fields!"

"Let's hit the remainder as they come out of the city then," said Davis. "The lead elements will have to be taken care of later."

Hartley brought the flight back to the east yet again and circled back to Bielefeld. On the approach to the city, the autobahn was a tight mass of tan vehicles pouring out into the fields beyond. With no AAA or SAMs to hit out at him, he reckoned it would be all too easy.

The radar warning receiver lit up.

"I've got bandits on our six!" said Martin. A second later, he heard Martin again. "Missile launch! I'm going evasive!"

Hartley's blood ran cold. He twisted his neck around, spotting several dots up high. Martin's Harrier swung left hard, dropping out a line of chaff and flare behind it.

"Shadow Flight, listen carefully," Hartley said. "We need to hit the mass of those vehicles as they're coming out of Bielefeld. Martin and Dunhill, continue on your run to the target. Sunshine, you're with me. Let's scatter those fighters."

"That missile came close!" said Martin. "I'm going for

the target now."

Hartley and Davis kept low to the ground, hoping to confuse any enemy air-to-air missiles with ground clutter below them. The pair of Harriers were at full throttle.

Hartley's radar warning beeped in his ear. "Sunshine, someone's got a missile lock on me," he said.

"Roger that, engage defensive," said Davis.

"Negative," replied Hartley. "I'm staying on them. Listen, I've got the one in the middle, you take the one on the left. We'll get in close and use cannons on whoever's left."

The warning bells screamed at Hartley. "Missile inbound," he said. He kept the Harrier as low as he dared, skimming over the brush and weeds below. Hartley's HUD showed a radar lock on one of the inbound enemy aircraft. The word "SHOOT" flashed at him. He breathed hard and let off a Sidewinder. "Fox Two!" he shouted.

The AIM-9M missile trail left a stream of smoke behind it as it leapt outwards and upwards from Hartley's plane. Davis fired off his missile at one of the planes on the outside of the formation.

Hartley watched as his target shot upwards and twisted in an upwards spiral. The missile flew past the enemy aircraft. "Damn it," he said. Moments later, Davis called over his radio. "Got him! Splash one bandit!"

Hartley saw the little fireball wink in and out against the afternoons sky. "Good kill, Sunshine! Mine missed."

Now it was an even match of two-on-two. Hartley

hoped his final missile would find its mark. The enemy planes were less than a kilometer away still flying a thousand feet above Hartley and Davis.

"Stay low," said Hartley. "Going up to meet them is playing their game, remember?"

The two enemy aircraft shot by overhead. Hartley squinted as he peered up at them. "I have MiG-21s up there," he said.

Hartley steered the planes around and watched as the Fishbeds swooped down out of the sky. In a matter of seconds, they were above the Harriers. Hartley felt like a mouse in a field, ready to be picked off by a hawk. The only thing to do was to fly as low as he could go and turn back and forth, hoping to cause a miss. The tracer fire poured down along the side of his Harrier.

Hartley and Davis turned again to find the MiGs accelerating up again into the sky.

"They're going for another strafing run," said Hartley. "Get ready."

Davis called back. "Next time, I'll follow them up. Cover me."

Hartley couldn't believe what he was hearing. "Look, we've done all we can here. it's time we jettison and try to make our way back home now. Fun's over."

There was no time to argue. Hartley jettisoned his rocket pods. The little Harrier jumped up a dozen feet in the air, no longer fettered by the steel beasts that were nestled under its belly. Somewhere below, the rocket pods fell into a tiny hamlet, long ago abandoned by its inhabitants. "Drop your pods, Davis. That's an order!" said Hartley.

But his wingman had either not heard him or was no longer listening. The MiGs swung back around but this time ignored the two Harriers. Hartley watched in horror as they lined up behind Dunhill and Martin. Both Harriers were ready to fire their rockets at the British vehicles below.

"They're after the others," Hartley said. "Let's go! Come on!"

Hartley brought the Harrier's nose up as the MiGs sped by him from right to left. A MiG on afterburners versus a Harrier was a lot like a race car compared to a family saloon. Hartley cursed at his aircraft, wishing it would climb faster.

A few hundred feet behind Hartley, the fully loaded Harrier piloted by Davis was struggling along at a lower climb angle and speed. Hartley thought about ordering Davis to jettison but he had already loosed his two AiM-9 Sidewinders. Hartley was the only one with an air-to-air missile.

The lead MiG and his wingman closed in on Martin's Harrier. Hartley watched Martin roll hard left and the MiGs were forced to barrel roll to stay behind it. The lead MiG's tracers flashed by Martin in a long arc of green light. The rear MiG fired next after the lead pilot went vertical to avoid an overshoot. Hartley grunted in the middle of the turn as he felt the blood leave his head.

The AiM-9's radar locked up the lead MiG. The pilot had gone full afterburners as he climbed. The rear of the plane was visible in the Hartley's HUD. The little box on the HUD showed that the missile was ready to fire and the growl in Hartley's ear grew to a high-pitched tone. "I have tone! Fox Two!"

The remaining missile popped off Hartley's Harrier and soared upwards to meet the lead MiG. Seconds later, a little ball flashed and disappeared where the enemy jet had been. Hartley felt his muscles relax for a moment. He knew he was very likely an ace at this point but for now, the remaining MiG was pumping holes in his mate so it really didn't seem to matter.

Martin screamed over the radio. "He's all over me! Get this bastard off me now!"

Hartley watched the remaining MiG peel off to the right as Martin vectored the Harrier in the middle of a hard turn. The MiG tried to turn with him but went wide. By the time Martin turned back to get on the MiG's tail, his Harrier was already smoking. The thick black cloud poured out from his engine.

Hartley shouted. "You're smoking! Get the hell away from here!"

Dunhill came over the radio, his voice full of cool satisfaction. "I have ground hits on those tanks coming out of the city. Lots of secondaries from the looks of it."

Hartley brought his plane within cannon range of the MiG. It had circled around in a tight arc and resumed its pursuit of Martin's wounded Harrier. "Sunshine, I'm heading back to base. Keep that MiG off me until I can get out of here," he said.

Hartley watched the MiG speed off from his Harrier. He knew he was outmatched up here though not outnumbered. He thought of the British vehicles below still streaming towards the NATO rear. There was no choice left to but to stay and fight.

"Shadow this is Sunshine," said Davis. "Get him on the run and bring him straight towards me. I'll use my cannons and rockets."

Hartley keyed his mike twice to acknowledge. As Martin pulled away with the trail of smoke behind him, Hartley aimed his nose towards the wounded plane. "That should give him an irresistible target," he said.

It occurred to him suddenly that he had placed his life in the hands of Davis utterly. He recalled the punch he had received from him along with the angry invectives. If Davis wanted him dead, now was the time to commit the perfect crime. All it would take would be delaying his shot at the MiG by a few seconds. No one would question it.

He watched the rear-view mirror as the MiG grew closer on his tail. Behind the enemy aircraft, he saw Davis's Harrier catching up.

"Alright, the MiG's on you now. Just give me a few seconds to get in position," Davis said.

Hartley jinked his Harrier but kept his speed constant. The first of the tracers whizzed by him. There were several loud knocks on the back of the plane.

The central warning panel lit up. Hartley's spirit sank and he put one hand on the ejection handle. If he survived this, he would find his way back to base and put Davis away for the rest of his days - war or no war.

Davis shouted. "Pull up! Pull up now!"

Hartley yanked the flight stick back, hoping the plane would respond. It angled up sharply and in the rear-view mirror, he saw the trail of SNEB rockets shoot past just below him, passing right through the spot where his Harrier had been only a moment ago. He looked back as he pulled tight and saw a black cloud where the MiG had been flying.

"Splash one bandit!" shouted Davis. Hartley was elated.

The MiGs were gone and now it was open season on the British army vehicles passing below.

"Gentlemen, we have a problem," said Hartley. "We appear to be out of air-to-ground ordnance."

There was a silence over the radio for a moment. Hartley checked his warning panel. It was all orange. No major damage to report. His Harrier would fly for the foreseeable future, but it would be wise to get home.

"We have helos coming in less than a minute," said Davis. "Let's check for artillery availability. There must be something. Hartley, you get home. I'll call it in on those bastards below."

Hartley was stunned into silence. Where the hell had Davis gone? Had he been replaced while Hartley wasn't looking? The man was famous for never sticking his neck out for anything. Even in training, he was the first one to call abort on anything less than a perfect run on a target.

Hartley looked at his gauges and watched Martin ahead of him. They were both damaged and it was time to go home.

"Roger, Sunshine," said Hartley. "We'll see you back at base."

Dunhill and Davis circled high over the British vehicles. The American helicopters came in low and delivered their rockets and anti-tank missiles. Ten minutes of death and fire and chaos ensued.

When the helicopters left, at least half the vehicles were destroyed or dispersed. Davis requested and received artillery support that broke the second wave of the remaining vehicles.

By the time they returned to the Harrier hide near Munster, the real British Army was able to destroy the Scimitars with carefully deployed anti-tank missiles that were watching for the encroaching enemy.

Hartley shook Davis's hand as he climbed out of the Harrier.

"Once they lost the element of surprise and took a proper hiding, it was over fairly quickly," shrugged Davis.

Hartley patted him on the shoulder. "I suppose you'll be wanting a promotion now that you've found your tempo out there."

Davis smiled. "I'll leave the leading to you from now on," he said. "Looks like you've got the knack for it."

Martin examined the damage on his Harrier. The engine had been shot up quite badly and the turbine would need to be replaced for it to work properly again. The ground technicians clearly had their work cut out for them.

Dunhill landed his Harrier. The jet was without a

scratch. The empty rocket pods were a testament to the destruction he had rained down on the Soviets in the POMCUS armored vehicles.

17

The clearing was full of activity. Aircraft technicians raced back and forth, carting spare parts to the aircraft and discarding the broken and damaged parts of the Harriers. Intelligence and air operations officers stepped in and out of the Marshall Cabins that sat on the grass.

Hartley smoked a cigarette, letting the fatigue wash over him. So much had already happened to him and his men and it was only the first day of the war. When he sat down to eat his field rations, he expected that his appetite wouldn't bear it. But instead he wolfed down the sandwich and the pasta. It was strangely satisfying to do something as simple as eat given how complex the rest of the day had been.

Davis joked around with Dunhill and Martin a little. The men even started kicking back and forth a football. When the major tapped Hartley on the shoulder, he simply dropped the cigarette at his feet and breathed out a long stream of smoke from his mouth before slowly getting up and walking to the cabin.

He plopped down on the hard metal chair. The maps of NORTHAG's front were taped up all around like wallpaper. Hartley didn't even need to look. He knew it was bad already.

What have you got?" he asked.

Briscoe sat down across from him and Hartley waved off the cup of tea he offered.

"Your two mates have been found. Stewart didn't make it. KIA," Briscoe said. Hartley reached for the cup of tea beside him.

"What about Spencer?"

"Managed to pull him out with nothing more than a sprained ankle," said Briscoe. "He's at field hospital right now near Rammstein. I expect he'll be back here in a couple of days if all goes well enough."

Hartley smiled as the Earl Grey fell down his throat. "Well, at least there's that," he said. "To Stewart." He clinked his thermos cup against Briscoe's. It was silent for a moment.

"All quiet on the western front?" asked Hartley. He pointed up towards the maps. One of them showed the area around Hannover completely encircled by red pins.

"Quite," said Briscoe with a smirk. He stood up and pointed to the maps. The red arrows that showed the enemy advance were near the Weser River. The blue NATO unit locations were all to the west of it.

"We've orchestrated a somewhat organized pull back towards the west," said Briscoe. "At this point, the Soviets are sending in their second echelon units or what's left of them after we hit their marshalling yards earlier today."

"Is Hannover under Soviet control now?" he asked.

Briscoe shook his head. "Elements of 1st Armored Division are inside the city," he said. "The Soviets sent in two regiments late this afternoon and were sent out packing. It looks like Ivan's leaving the city alone and bypassing it for now. If I were a betting man, the Poles will be sent into the meat grinder when they arrive at the front."

"We need you up there again tonight," said Briscoe. "The whole squadron is going up. Number 4 too."

Briscoe pointed to the blurred recon photos of several large bridges. "I suppose you'll be needing those taken care of at some point?" he asked.

"Three major bridges west of Hannover," said Briscoe. "German engineers blew most of the bridges going across the Weser about half an hour ago. The Russians will be using these remaining bridges to help their tanks and men cross the river. We've left these bridges intact to blow them at just the right time and cause massive chaos."

Hartley plucked the photo from the wall and tried to remember the appearance of the bridges. "And you want us to go out in the dark and perform this mission with no night capability?"

Briscoe nodded. "That's exactly it," he said. "We've got hold of some newer Harriers based on the GR.7 upgrade. You'll be flying those. For the pilots, everything is nearly the same in the cockpit except for the ability to operate at night with night vision goggles."

Hartley nearly dropped his tea. "Any time to familiarize with it?" he asked.

"You'll have to do it on your way to the target," said Briscoe. "Once you get there, you'll have ground forces illuminating the target for your Paveway IIs. Your guided bombs will ride the laser down directly to the bridges."

"Will we have air cover this time?" Hartley asked. "Proper air cover?"

Briscoe sniffed. "This time you'll have an entire squadron of F-15s from Bitburg over you," he said. "They've been escorting offensive counter-air missions all day. The presence of enemy fighters in theater has dwindled to about a quarter of what it was this morning."

Hartley had heard that before. His bigger worry was the AAA and SAMs. The "low and slow" approach over the target had cost them all dearly today.

"Air defense suppression?" asked Hartley.

"Artillery and air," said Briscoe. "There are two SEAD flights going in two minutes before your run. American F-4G Phantoms from Spangdahlem."

Hartley looked over the list of mission names and callsigns. It all looked very solid but of course lots of moving parts meant the potential for something to go wrong. Three men had already been lost and four Harriers were gone in a single day. How much more could they take?

"When do we get replacements?" he asked Briscoe.

"Tomorrow morning," came the reply.

Hartley set his tea down. "You mean to tell me this is it?" he asked.

Briscoe nodded. "Until tomorrow, you'll need to wait. It's what everyone else is doing."

Hartley felt like today was a series of gut punches. The Red Flag exercises tried to impart a sense of how dangerous the battlefield could be, but it had never really sunk in properly until the real thing hit. He staggered out of the Marshall Cabin and gathered the others around him to go over the mission.

Twenty minutes later, he was back up in the air. It was pitch-black outside and the clouds high above blotted out the stars. He watched the screen on his navigation system. He was a little happier to be away from all the nonsense on the ground.

Retreats, feints, withdrawals...the big picture seemed to matter less and less to him as the day went on. Every mission now was simply a matter of survival. Somewhere out there in the dark were three targets just waiting to be hit.

18

"I've always hated wearing these goggles," said Dunhill.

Hartley pushed up on the throttle. The big Paveway laser-guided bombs were monsters at 1,000 pounds each. For larger planes, it was tough to carry but for a smaller single-engine aircraft like the Harrier, it was like telling a six-year old to lug around grandmother's packed suitcase through the airport.

"Well I'd say it's a damn sight better than crashing into a hillside," replied Davis.

The German plain passed by below them, lit up as a neutral green through the filters and electronics of the night vision goggles.

"Let's keep things a bit higher than we usually fly," said Hartley. He knew there was a certain element of distortion with the goggles - not too much but enough that warranted avoiding the risks of flying low. Ahead of him, he could see the bright blinding flash of artillery being fired on the ground.

"Looks like they're busy tonight down there," said Martin. "I heard the Soviets are awful at operating during the night."

"Something's not right," said Dunhill. "My engine…"

Hartley turned to look back at Dunhill's plane. The left intake glowed a fiery orange-red. "Looks like you've taken in something," he said to Dunhill.

"Roger that, probably a bird strike," he replied. "I might be okay for a while though. Let's see."

Hartley felt a surge of anger course through him. "That's enough. You're RTB, mate. That's an order."

Dunhill's Harrier peeled off out of formation and returned south towards the hide. "Alright, gents," said Hartley to the formation. "Three planes. Three targets. Let's make those bombs count."

The conversation was cut short as the remaining Harriers in their squadron along with number 4 squadron jostled into formation. The assignment was clear cut.

The number 3 squadron would be hitting the bridges and the Harriers in number 4 would be dropping cluster bombs on the troops and tanks that were bunched up on the east bank, waiting to cross. A few of the Harriers were fitted with infrared reconnaissance pods that would perform bomb damage assessment.

Below them, the Weser River snaked through northern Germany all the way to the port city of Bremen.

Hartley's Harrier began to shudder as he reached 600

knots. He reckoned it was the weight of the Paveways he was carrying and tried his best to simply ignore it. Dropping out of formation so close to the target would be bad form.

The radar warning receiver began to chirp. Hartley heard Martin call out the bogeys high above them.

"Should be the F-4s coming back now," said Davis. Hartley hoped he was right. He checked the IFF and felt a huge weight drop off his shoulders as it responded with the right tone.

"The artillery should be landing right about now," said Hartley. "Turn on your lasers."

Hartley reached over in the cockpit and changed the heads-up display mode. The HUD showed the distance and range to the first bridge. Closing rapidly towards it, he looked down at the inky black of the river below and hoped he would return home soon. All he wanted to do right now was catch some sleep.

The bridge came into view far in the distance. Small arms tracers flew towards his cockpit and spit erratically along his flight path.

Hartley pulled back on the flight stick and followed the line on the HUD to correct his angle of attack and bearing to the target. As he climbed up past one thousand feet, he felt the Harrier tremble.

The radar warning receiver chirped again and again, telling him of the enemy radars all around. Never had he felt so vulnerable in all his life. The feeling was remarkably like being naked in a room filled with an angry mob.

The HUD symbols showed a square around the bridge where the ground forces were illuminating the target. "Paveway!" Hartley cried. The Harrier's engines whined as the bombs released from the Harrier's underbelly. The radar warning rang its alarm. Somewhere out there were two enemy SAMs heading straight for his plane.

"SAM launch!" Hartley shouted into his mike. He drove the nose of the Harrier down, aiming for the ground. He gulped as the plane pulled up level just above the crestline of a low hill.

The forward air controller's voice came over the radio seconds later. "Nice hit! You were right on target!" he shouted. Hartley swerved around another low hill on the west bank and settled the plane low over the Weser. The radar warning receiver had stopped its bleating. Hartley let a long breath come out. "I think I lost those SAMs," he said.

Hartley steered his Harrier towards the west bank of the Weser and out of reach of the enemy anti-aircraft artillery. On the opposite bank, the Harriers from Number 4 squadron were dropping their cluster munitions on the assembled enemy tanks and men waiting to cross the river. The munitions burst behind the planes, leaving behind a long sheet of flame draped over the landscape.

"Alright, Davis get this right. Drop when ready," said Hartley.

Davis's Harrier was now flying low over the waters of the Weser River. The Harrier shot through an opening left between the demolished span that connected the little towns of Stolzenau on the west and Leese to the east. The second target bridge was coming up in a little over two miles near Landesbergen

"I have it in sight," Davis announced. "Request sparkle. Almost there...something's not right, dammit!!"

The sound of static and a tinny voice sounded faintly in Hartley's ear. "Shadow, our ground forces ran into a little trouble on the way to the target. They need more time."

"Hell!" shouted Hartley. "The radar warning receiver was already lit up. Davis was taking fire from the eastern bank and the bridge ahead.

"Shadow to Sunshine, abort your run," Hartley said. "I say again, abort. The ground troops are not in place to lase the target."

A line of anti-aircraft tracers buzzed over the top of Davis's Harrier. He banked left and swung into formation with Hartley and the other Harriers on the western bank. He watched as a pair of missiles lashed out from the opposite bank and slammed into a pair of Harriers from Number 4 squadron as they dropped their cluster munitions on the teeming mass of enemy vehicles and men waiting to cross the bridge.

"We keep on to the next bridge then," said Hartley. "Stay tight and watch the ground."

The final bridge was thirty miles to the north. It was a long low bridge running south of Uesen. The Harriers flew north and followed the river, making a sharp turn to the west along with it. At the turn, the anti-aircraft fire and small arms fire was thick as Martin's Harrier faced the enemy troops head on.

"I'm taking hits!" he shouted.

Hartley closed his eyes and hoped Martin would make it out. Getting hit with a pair of 1,000-pound bombs strapped to your undercarriage and a full load of fuel was unnerving to say the least. A lesser man would have cracked but Martin kept his course and rolled to his left. His Harrier leapt up into the night at full throttle.

"Paveway!" Martin shouted. The bombs fell swiftly and silently down into the night, guided by the invisible laser below. Watching from the west, he saw the explosion on the bridge. It looked like it was closer to the east end of it rather than in the middle.

Hartley doubted whether it was a direct hit. There was no use in telling Martin about it now. They would all find out in the morning after bomb damage assessment had been performed.

"I don't think it's a clean hit," said Davis. "I'm not sure though."

"What?!" cried Martin.

Hartley cursed Davis's brutal honesty in the moment. Still, he knew he was probably right.

"Alright, gentlemen, it's time to get home now," said Hartley. "We've had our fun for the evening."

"I think you've forgotten the second bridge," said Davis. "It's still up."

"You've got to be mad!" shouted Hartley.

They were heading back south now. They could certainly make a run on the second bridge but with the element of surprise gone, it would be the closest thing to suicide that he had seen so far today.

"Shadow Flight, this is Team Two," Hartley heard over the radio. "We are in position now and have painted the target."

"That's it! I'm going for it with or without you," said Davis. "You might as well keep me company."

Hartley shook his head. "I'd order a return to base but I'm not sure what good it would do," he said.

Somewhere in the night, several Soviet regiments were rushing across the second bridge over the Weser River. Each enemy that got through was another potential hole in NATO's defense. Hartley knew there was simply no choice. The enemy was alerted and ready for them. It was going to be nasty.

"Alright, Davis goes down the middle while the rest of us go down the west bank. Use your cannons to suppress any anti-air down there," said Hartley.

"Hope those Number 4 boys did a good enough job with those clusters," said Martin.

Hartley shook his head. "Look, it's very likely that at least someone is alive down there and angry enough to shoot back," he said. "Just make a quick pass. Follow me in, Martin. Good luck, Davis."

Hartley shoved the throttle lever forward. Martin's plane fell in behind him and to the right. If the timing worked out right, they would be over the eastern portion of the bank thirty seconds before Davis started his run. With any luck, the SAMs and AAA wouldn't even notice him. It seemed too much to hope for, but Hartley grasped at anything at all.

Through his night vision goggles, he spotted the bridge in the distance. Dark shapes moved over it briskly, racing from left to right. There were several fires burning on the east side of the bank where the Soviet vehicles had been hit with cluster munitions. Bright intense green spots flared up in his field of vision where vehicles exploded.

The radar warning receiver blared in his ears. Hartley brought his Harrier up to five hundred feet and banked hard to the left, hoping that whatever missile was coming would pass by.

Dropping the chaff and flare behind him, he pointed the nozzles to the rear and fired them on a tight turn. The aircraft vectored hard right. Something passed by him on the left.

"Okay, well, there's definitely one SAM out there still operating!" said Hartley.

They flew over a densely concentrated group of vehicles at their 11 o'clock. Hartley fired a burst from the ADEN cannons. Martin did the same. The smoke drifted upwards and obscured Hartley's view.

"I'm blind here!" Martin shouted.

"Use your instruments!" shouted Hartley. "Get low and fly straight. There are no mountains around here!"

A series of low thuds sounded along the bottom of Hartley's aircraft. He reached over and flicked off the lights of the central warning system. His Harrier passed through the cloud of smoke. In front of him was a cracked cockpit window.

"How are we doing back there?" he shouted back to Martin. No response. Hartley looked to his right and saw the Harrier go down into the river. A high jet of water flew up where the plane crashed and broke apart.

Hartley turned again, facing the cloud of smoke he had just emerged from.

"I'm going in now!" shouted Davis. "Target's painted!" The Harrier shot up suddenly about a mile from the bridge. Hartley fired his cannons again, hoping to keep the enemy heads down just long enough.

A second later, he heard Davis shout. "Paveway!"

The bombs slid off the belly of the Harrier. Davis kept his nose and angle of attack high enough to help the bomb in. Moments later, the bridge to his left shook with the sudden impact of the thousand-pound Paveways. The explosion sent ripples down both ends of the bridge and the main supports collapsed completely into the water below.

Hartley's finger depressed the trigger on the flight stick despite the fact he had run out of ammunition at least ten seconds ago. The radar warning receiver was silent, but it was time. Time to get the hell out of there.

"Let's go, Davis," said Hartley. "We better head back now."

On the way home, Hartley thought about Martin. Like so many of the other pilots, he was a young man full of hopes and dreams. When he had come to the squadron fresh-faced only six months ago, he brought a much-needed breath of energy to Shadow Flight.

Hartley's mind drifted to the letters he would be writing to parents and wives soon. He resolved to get to them before bed. But as soon as he sat down in the tent, his eyes closed and he woke up in the darkness with his head on the desk an hour later.

The papers were still blank.

19

The next morning came and with it were new pilots. Jameson, Harris, and Foote were Harrier trainers back in England. They were older men with flight experience who weren't too eager to see combat but who weren't afraid of it either.

Hartley shook their hands and noted the look of - what? - pity, awe, envy that they had for him and Davis and Dunhill. The three men had been tested in combat and had formed a brotherhood that was forged in the blood and death and daring of war.

They were quiet as they waited for the new Harriers to arrive at the hide. Hartley tried to think of something to say to them. He thought of the papers that awaited him and the letters he would need to write. He realized that he would need to do it soon before he too became the subject of a letter. If yesterday was anything to go by, that could be any time at all.

He stumbled over what to say about each man. Davis entered the tent.

"Harriers are here," Davis said. "More replacement pilots too."

Hartley grunted and fumbled with the pen, staring down at the paper filled with muddled sentences and half-baked sentiments.

Davis saw the sour look on Hartley face. "Hell of day wasn't it?" he said.

"How the hell do you do it all justice?" Hartley said. "Martin, Stewart, Nelson, Bellamy...what do you say about these men?"

Davis shrugged and sat down. "I've written one of those before. Just after the accident," he said. "There are no rules to this. You just...say what you feel. Be honest."

Hartley nodded and pulled out a new piece of paper. Davis picked up the crumpled sheets that lay on the floor of the tent and threw them in the nearby bin. Then he left Hartley alone.

The words rushed into Hartley's head as fast as the tears spilled out. Hartley picked out the best memories he could. There were the barbecues and the pick-up games of football in the sun, Stewart's turns of phrases when he was angry, and the days spent doing nothing together but waiting for a mission. It was all there stored away inside him. All he needed to do was unlock it.

By the time, the final letter was written and signed, Hartley was smiling and chuckling to himself. The day was new and with it came the prospect of life and death, moments to be grasped and horrors to be forgotten.

It was his life now. And he was proud to spend it with men like these.

ABOUT THE AUTHOR

Brad Smith is a Canadian author living in rural Japan. He works as a game designer as well as a writer. You can check out his blog at: www.hexsides.com

BRAD SMITH

Printed in Great Britain
by Amazon